STILL THE ONE

A SPICY LATER IN LIFE ROMANCE SERIES

STILLWATER SPRINGS
BOOK ONE

JEM JOHNSON

THOSE JOHNSON GIRLS

The two-lane road stretched in front of me like a broken lifeline. The faded yellow was jagged and cracked against the black of the asphalt. Hills rolled gentle and green on the horizon. Barns slouched in various states of decay, and cows ignored me as I sped past. The windows of my SUV were cracked just enough to let in air and dust and the faint smell of cut grass.

God, I loved driving. It was the only time I could simply be. No one could reasonably expect me to answer emails or call them back when I was on the road. Hands-free laws were my religion. My phone was face-down in the passenger seat, and for once, I didn't feel guilty about ignoring it.

Instead, I had a spicy little romantasy piping

through the speakers. The deep, brooding British narrator was doing his damnedest to make Fae King Kairon sound sexy and not... vaguely predatory.

"You're mine now, little mortal," the narrator growled, drawing out every syllable like foreplay. "I'll make you scream until you remember nothing of the world you left behind. Only me. Only this."

I scrunched my nose. "Little mortal? She's twenty-two and can't boil pasta without calling her mom."

The heroine whimpered. Or rather, the female narrator did, breathy and high-pitched, like she'd just discovered both sex and adjectives in the same sentence.

"I shouldn't want this," the girl gasped. "You're my enemy. My captor. But your fingers feel like... sunlight and sin."

I snorted. "Sunlight and sin. Jesus."

To be fair, I knew exactly what this book was. It was at the top of the charts. Number one in roman-tasy, complete with a dagger-wielding cover model who probably bench-pressed mountains in his spare time. Honestly? I was listening for this part. Not the *Chosen One* prophecy, or the kingdom politics, or the heroine's breathless revelations about her *inner power*.

No, I was here for the tension. The slow burn. The spicy payoff.

As an author myself, I didn't write fae kings or magical wars. I wrote about flannel-wearing handymen with big hands and bad communication skills. But under the surface? My books weren't all that different. They were filled with women like me who wanted to be seen. Wanted to be chosen. Wanted to be touched in ways they weren't in their real life. Women who were wanted.

The audiobook swelled with moans and groans. An ancient tongue taking a trip down south when—

Riiiiiiing!

I jumped, hands jerking on the wheel. The Bluetooth kicked in, cutting off whatever Kairon was about to do with the heroine's "velvet darkness" and replaced it with the all-too-familiar ringtone I'd assigned to my son.

Of course.

It had been Zach who had shown me how to mute my calls except for the important ones. His number being one of the few exceptions.

I glanced down. His name blinked across the dash, innocuous and inevitable. I exhaled slowly through my nose, thumb hovering over the steering wheel's hands-free button. I didn't answer yet. I just stared at his name and let the silence stretch.

Just ten more minutes. Ten more minutes of fae kings and fantasy and the illusion that someone like me could still be the center of a story.

But that wasn't how life worked.

I hit accept.

"Hey, buddy." My voice was smooth like a tablecloth over a messy kitchen. "How's your day going?"

"Not going great, Mom." Zach's voice was tight. Too fast. That upper register he hit when anxiety curled around his throat and wouldn't let go.

I glanced at the time on the dash. "You're not supposed to be at the interview for another thirty minutes."

"I know, I know. But I'm freaking out." A pause. Breathing. Shuffling. "I can't feel my hands."

"Can you still drive the car?"

"Barely."

I took a deep breath and let it out slowly, hoping he would double my behavior and do the same. "Maybe take a rideshare so you don't kill yourself trying to be employable."

"I overdrew my account by five bucks last night when I stopped at the gas station."

I had seen that charge. It hadn't been for gas. My

son used fumes of a different variety to help his anxiety when it got a little too out of hand. Which was more and more frequent.

"Zach, listen to me. You are going to be fine. You're qualified. You're capable. You are—"

"A mess."

"A lovable mess."

He groaned. "I'm gonna bomb it."

"You are not. You're smart. You've got experience."

"I slung popcorn at the local movie theater in high school."

"And you were employee of the month twice. Besides, you're a mediocre white man. Statistically, this job is yours."

"I'm only half white."

"Half is more than enough. The privilege kicks in by age six."

That got a laugh out of him. A real one. I could hear the fear loosening its grip just enough to let the oxygen back in.

"I don't know, Mom. I don't feel like I belong in places like that."

"None of us do, honey. The secret is to pretend you do until you're too valuable to ignore. You're a Gen Z miracle. You care, and you show up. That's already more than half of what the rest of the work-force is capable of."

"Are you gonna give me your 'Gen X parents were forged in chaos' speech again?"

"No, that's only for when you forget how to change a tire or call me crying about doing your taxes. This is just a standard maternal pep talk."

Another pause. The silence stretched. I knew what was coming before he said it.

"Dad never called me back."

I didn't answer. My grip on the steering wheel tightened. My shoulders did that thing they always did when my ex-husband came up. They locked up like they were bracing for impact.

"He said he'd help me prep for this interview," Zach went on. "Said he had contacts at the company. Then poof. Ghosted."

I still didn't say anything.

"Classic, right?"

Yeah, classic. But I held my tongue.

It wasn't anger I felt. Not really. Anger had already burned through me and left ash behind. This was something heavier and less righteous. Like watching a car wreck in slow motion when you knew the brakes were faulty.

I'd had that feeling at the beginning of my relationship with Greg McNaulty. A whisper in my gut I kept trying to shush. That Greg would never really show up for Zach, because he'd never truly shown up for me. Sure, he'd been physically present. But rarely mentally present. And never emotionally present. The fact that we'd made it twenty-two years before it all fell apart felt less like a triumph and more like a delay of the inevitable. And even that… our divorce… I'd seen it coming, hadn't I?

"Can you call him?" Zach asked.

I swallowed hard. My stomach turned over like I'd swallowed a rock.

"I just want to make sure he called his contact. Might be the only time I get to use nepotism."

I knew how much this job meant to Zach. Which meant it meant a lot to me. I'd had a couple of months as a true empty nester. No kid and no husband, since Greg had left the day after Zach graduated college. Though my divorce was embarrassing, the freedom and joy of having my own place to myself was exhilarating. I wasn't quite ready to give that up. I'd have to if my son, who couldn't keep his checking account balanced, didn't get this job that in truth he wasn't quite as qualified as I'd just insisted he was.

"Sure, I'll call him."

"You will?"

"Yeah. I've got it, buddy."

It was a reflex, the way I said it. The way I always said it. *I've got it.* Like my whole life was one long game of catch and no one ever thought to ask if I wanted to drop the damn ball.

My baby boy thanked me and told me he loved me. I said it back, meaning every word. We hung up.

A few more miles of cracked pavement passed beneath my tires. Fields blurred to my left, an old tractor rusting under the weight of memory to my right. I let the scenery work on me, let it seep into the cracks. It didn't fix anything, but at least it didn't ask anything of me.

I turned the audiobook back on. The fae king was back at it, kissing some part of the heroine that should've made me tingle where my butt hit the leather seat warmer.

"You taste like starlight and danger," the fae king growled. Just as she gasped his name, the door flew open and—

"Kairon," came a new voice. "I see you haven't changed."

The old lover. Of course.

I groaned and shut the sound off. The fantasy

world had become a little too on the nose for my liking.

I punched in the code for my ex-husband's number. Each digit felt heavier than the last.

It rang.

Once.

Twice.

Three times.

Then it picked up.

And I braced. Not for the conversation. Greg wasn't a talker. I'd carry the conversation, like always. Ask him to do what he promised, which would sound like me nagging in his ears. But fiction wasn't done having its fun with me today. Like the fae king, the person on the other end of the line was an unexpected intruder.

"Hello?" The voice was soft and syrupy, with a little bow of polite surprise on the end. "This is Kelly."

Of course, it was.

I blinked at the windshield. The world outside had gone static. Just cornfields and disappointment rolling past in golden rows.

"Hi, Kelly. It's Celia."

A beat of silence.

Then, "Oh. Hi." Her voice tightened just enough to notice. "What can I do for you, Celia?"

"Is Greg available?"

"He's… around. But he can't come to the phone."

I exhaled, slow and careful. "I'm calling for Zach. He has a job interview today. Greg said he'd make a call to someone at the company to put in a good word for his son, but Zach hasn't heard anything from him."

Another pause. This one longer. Then: "Couldn't Zach call himself?"

"He did call his dad," I said, a bit sharper now. "Greg didn't answer. Didn't call back. So now it's me." Because when things don't get handled, I handle them. I would call the contact myself… if I knew their name.

"Well," Kelly said, her voice lifting into that faux-cheerful lilt that always meant she was winding up for a dig, "if Greg said he would, then he did. He always keeps his word."

The laugh that came out of me wasn't kind. "Yeah. He sure does."

Click. Just like that, she was gone.

I stared at the call screen for half a second before picking up the phone and throwing it—hard—

against the dash. It bounced off the console and thudded to the floor like a dead thing.

And then—sirens.

The lights hit my rearview mirror in flashing red and blue. I groaned as I pulled to the shoulder, gravel crackling under my tires. The cop car slid in behind me like a judgment. I rolled down the window as the officer approached, still fuming, still rattled, still trying to crawl out of the hole in my chest that phone call had carved open.

"License and registration, ma'am. I pulled you over for cell phone use while driving."

"I wasn't on the phone. I threw it."

The cop raised an eyebrow.

"I threw it across the car. Out of exasperation."

He didn't even blink. Just took my license, walked back to his cruiser, and left me there with my heartbeat tapping against the inside of my throat.

When he returned, he handed me a slip of paper and said, "You can contest the ticket in court if you want. But around here, we take distracted driving seriously."

I took the paper in silence. I didn't trust myself to open my mouth.

He squinted at my license again, then at my face. "Wait a minute. Celia Hart? Is that you?"

I would've perked up and smiled. But I didn't recognize this man from my childhood. He was younger than me. Which had to mean he had a very different impression of me than the people I had grown up with in Stillwater Creek.

"I thought you left town for good. Lotta folks'll be interested to hear you're back. Some of 'em still think you ruined half this place with that book you wrote."

His grin was polite. His tone wasn't.

"Anyway. Welcome home." He tipped his hat like he was doing me a favor and walked off.

I looked at the ticket.

Then at the steering wheel.

Then at the cracked phone on the floorboard.

I sat there, engine idling, blinking at the sunlight, wondering if coming back had been a mistake. Not because of what I might find when I went into my hometown. Because I was already losing myself again.

CHAPTER TWO

Stillwater Springs looked like someone had run a Restoration Hardware catalog through a time machine, slapped on a few solar panels, and called it progress.

There were more streetlights than I remembered. Brighter ones, too. The kind that didn't buzz or flicker or turn every mosquito into a kamikaze pilot. A new crosswalk by the library flashed a polite strobe when someone stepped onto it. But the old gas station where we used to buy contraband Mountain Dew and frozen burritos at midnight? Gone. Now it was a Starbucks with a patio and drive-thru, right across from the original soda fountain that had somehow survived a century.

I slowed as I passed the town square. The bones

were still the same: brick storefronts, the clock tower, Mr. Abernathy's barbershop that probably still smelled like Old Spice and mildew. But nestled between the hardware store and the corner bakery was a glossy boutique with white walls and matte gold fixtures. "Curated goods," the sign read. Whatever that meant. I had a sneaking suspicion it involved twenty-eight-dollar candles and people saying "aesthetic" as a noun.

The town had tried to resist change. God, how they'd fought. Zoning meetings, angry letters to the editor, yard signs declaring *Keep Stillwater Pure*. Unfortunately, evolution is the first law of the universe—adapt or die. Stillwater had come close to the latter.

Most of us youth (or who had once been youth) left as soon as we could. College, military, jobs, anywhere but here. Who wanted to stay in a town stuck in the *Leave It to Beaver* era, complete with its gender roles, church picnics, and a gossip pipeline strong enough to put the NSA to shame?

A few had stayed. Fewer had come back. Or so I thought.

As I rolled down Main Street, I saw familiar faces. Not names, not yet. Just glimpses. Laugh lines that had deepened. Hairlines that had retreated.

Bodies that had softened or hardened in ways life demands. People I once passed in hallways and yearbooks now leaned against brick buildings sipping matcha or pushed strollers past the playground where the bad boys—like the really bad boy, Jamie Tarley—used to smoke behind the middle school playground.

I kept my sunglasses on. Tinted windows up. Air conditioning set to "avoid eye contact."

It wasn't that I was a celebrity here. I hadn't been homecoming queen or prom royalty. I'd been one B away from class valedictorian and was voted "Most Likely to Succeed." Depending on who you asked, I had either lived up to that or spectacularly betrayed it.

I'd written books. A whole series of them. Bestsellers, technically. Small-town romances full of cinnamon roll men and women who baked their way into emotional security. Yes, the fictional town was loosely inspired by Stillwater. Yes, it had the same courthouse, same creek, same charming general store that always seemed to carry just the right thing at the right moment.

But it was idealized. An embroidered version of reality. I'd swapped out the classicism and misogyny for quilting bees and found family. Taken creative license with geography. Apparently, that hadn't stopped tourists from showing up expecting cobblestone streets and spontaneous pie contests.

I passed a banner stretched across the bank: *Take the Stillwater Stories Walking Tour – as featured in the bestselling books by Celia Hart.*

I slid even lower in my seat.

There had been a time when seeing my name on a banner like that might've made me proud. Or at least amused. Right now, all it did was make my stomach flip.

The truth was, I hadn't written anything new in over a year. Not anything romantic anyway. For some reason, people kept getting murdered in the first chapter of every manuscript I started.

Finally, I turned off the main road, past the little league fields where I'd struck out in sports and romance, and the church where I nearly fainted once from wearing Spanx in August. I didn't even glance at my old high school. I wasn't ready to face those memories anytime soon.

The house looked the same. White clapboard, green shutters, the screen door with a tear in the bottom right corner where the dog used to nose her way in. The porch swing still creaked gently in the breeze, like it had been waiting for someone to come home.

I pulled into the gravel driveway and parked, leaving the engine running a moment longer than I needed to. I just sat there, fingers on the wheel, letting the hum of the car hold me together a few seconds more.

Then I killed the engine, grabbed my bag, and stepped out. Only to stop in my tracks. I hadn't even made it to the front door.

I was still standing in the driveway, hand resting on the roof of my SUV, when I saw them.

Two figures, walking side by side down the opposite sidewalk like it was any old Tuesday, and they weren't part of my personal mythology.

Tessa Bloom floated—because that's what she did now. She floated. Flowy linen pants, gauzy wrap, and arms loose at her sides like she'd just stepped out of a catalog for coastal living and inner peace. Her hair, dark tight curls that reached for the sun in a salutation, shimmered like a halo she'd probably earned through breathwork and kale.

Beside her was Lana Russo, in jeans and a tank top that probably hadn't been ironed since the Bush administration, iced coffee in one hand and a tote bag slung over her shoulder like a badge of working motherhood. She was talking with her hands, walking fast, and probably solving a crisis with every step.

I froze. Half-behind my car, half-behind a mess of feelings I hadn't planned on unpacking just yet.

Tessa laughed at something Lana said. The sound drifted across the street like wind chimes in July.

God, I missed them.

Not just the two women walking toward the corner now—but us. The way we used to be. The way we'd held each other's secrets and covered for each other's lies. The way we swore—loudly and dramatically—that no matter where we went after graduation, we'd never lose touch.

And yet… here we were. Well, there they went, and here I was. By myself.

They turned the corner, chatting easily, a whole rhythm between them. Familiar. Comfortable. Lived-in.

They had moved back. When had that happened? Why hadn't I known?

Why were they hanging out without me?

I sank a little lower behind the SUV door, as if hiding from old friends was normal behavior for a grown woman with a mortgage, a flailing career, and a failed marriage under her belt.

Maybe they thought I'd outgrown them. Or maybe they'd outgrown me. Tessa had become a soft-spoken oracle, and Lana was still holding everyone's life together with nothing but caffeine and rage. And me? I'd written books about women like them who stuck together without ever telling them they were the blueprint. I'd fictionalized our friendship, polished it up, given it a happy ending.

Real life hadn't cooperated.

I watched them laugh again, something low and easy, and something sharp tugged at my chest. Jealousy maybe. Grief, probably. Sometimes they wore the same coat.

Tessa and Lana hadn't seen me. Or maybe they had, and they'd just kept walking. That thought stung more than I wanted to admit.

I turned toward the house before I could get caught out here like a soap opera character, leaning against a car and mourning a past I'd helped fracture.

The porch steps creaked under my weight like they remembered me. I opened the door, stepped inside, and shut it gently behind me.

The quiet that followed wasn't peaceful. It was chaos, holding its breath.

The house smelled wrong. Like something sour

had settled under the surface—spilled food, old paper, forgotten time. The hallway looked mostly untouched, but as I stepped farther in, the signs began to stack up.

A pile of mail had collapsed across the entry table, most of it unopened. Some envelopes were still rubber-banded together, like maybe he thought he'd get to them all at once. Catalogs and bills and junk from Medicare supplement companies that preyed on confusion.

In the living room, every lamp was on. All at once. It was the middle of the day, but they glowed like searchlights, throwing long, accusatory shadows over the mess.

There were cups in strange places—on the floor, the windowsill, the bookshelf. A plate balanced on the arm of the recliner, hardened scrambled eggs fossilized onto the surface. Blankets lay crumpled on the couch like he'd been sleeping there. The coffee table was covered in pill bottles, half-used tissues, and a mostly empty box of saltines.

The remote was taped together with masking tape. The TV was off, but the radio in the kitchen hummed faintly—jazz or maybe something trying to be.

I took a breath and stepped through to the

kitchen. That's where the worst of it hit. There was a blackened scar across one of the cabinet doors above the stove. The wall behind the range was scorched, and the ceiling was still stained with smoke residue. The fire hadn't spread, but it had tried.

The story came back to me in pieces. The neighbor had smelled the smoke. The fire department came. No one was hurt, but it was the final straw. That was when the call came. That was when the decision was made.

My dad had been moved into care while I was across the country finalizing the divorce and getting Zach settled. Too many loose ends, and I'd convinced myself—maybe others too—that he was doing okay.

He wasn't.

The man who used to rise before dawn to pack my lunch, who once drove four hours to sit in the front row of a regional spelling bee, who taught me how to hammer a nail and balance a checkbook and never forget birthdays… I hadn't been here. Not when it mattered.

I dropped my bag in the corner and started picking up the pieces. I tossed spoiled food, turned off lamps, rinsed crusted dishes. I wiped down countertops sticky with something sweet and unidentifiable. I scrubbed the table. Stacked the magazines. Pulled throw blankets into a basket. Bagged up the mail and marked it for sorting later.

I didn't cry. I was too busy making order out of the mess.

The first floor began to resemble something like normal again. Or at least, something like manageable. When I couldn't find another thing to straighten or disinfect, I made my way upstairs.

The carpet was still the same faded green it had always been. I skipped the door to my parents' room. I couldn't go in there yet. Couldn't see his slippers. Her perfume bottles that he'd never gotten rid of. The bed they'd shared, now empty and gathering dust.

Instead, I opened the door at the end of the hall.

My room.

It was... untouched.

The wallpaper—sun-faded florals I'd hated even when my mom had picked them, but I didn't want to upset her—still clung to the walls. My twin bed, still tucked in, military neat, the corners sharp from decades of habit. A bookshelf lined with paperbacks I hadn't touched since high school—*Sweet Valley High, The Outsiders*, a dog-eared copy of *The Bell Jar* that felt more like prophecy than literature.

My old corkboard still hung above the desk. Notes from Lana and Tessa, folded like origami. A xeroxed ticket from the senior play. My acceptance letter to Northwestern, a little yellowed with age. A photo of me and my two best girlfriends, the three of us, arms linked, wearing too much eyeliner and the same shade of confidence we hadn't yet learned how to hold.

There was a dried corsage hanging on the wall, too. From junior prom. I hadn't gone to the dance, but my next-door neighbor had given it to me. Wrapped in tissue paper with a note: *Save a dance for me.*

I moved toward the window and pushed it open, letting the warm, late-afternoon air roll in. The screen stuck, then gave way with a creak. The breeze carried the scent of honeysuckle and mown grass and the sound of birds arguing in the hedge below.

I looked up. And there he was. Bo Porter was standing in the window of the house across the yard. He was in his window, the one that faced mine since we were both in the crib and likely had answered each other's cries. The one he used to throw small pebbles from, just soft enough to ping but not shatter.

He was looking at me.

Just looking.

No wave. No smile. No gesture.

His face looked older. Grayer at the temples. But still solid, still steady.

And still Bo.

My heart came to a complete stop. Or maybe it started beating again. It was hard to tell. The noise in my chest was the kind that only came from things that had been buried too long.

I didn't look away. I didn't hide. I couldn't. He'd already seen me. And this part of my past that I'd run away from was going to demand an answer.

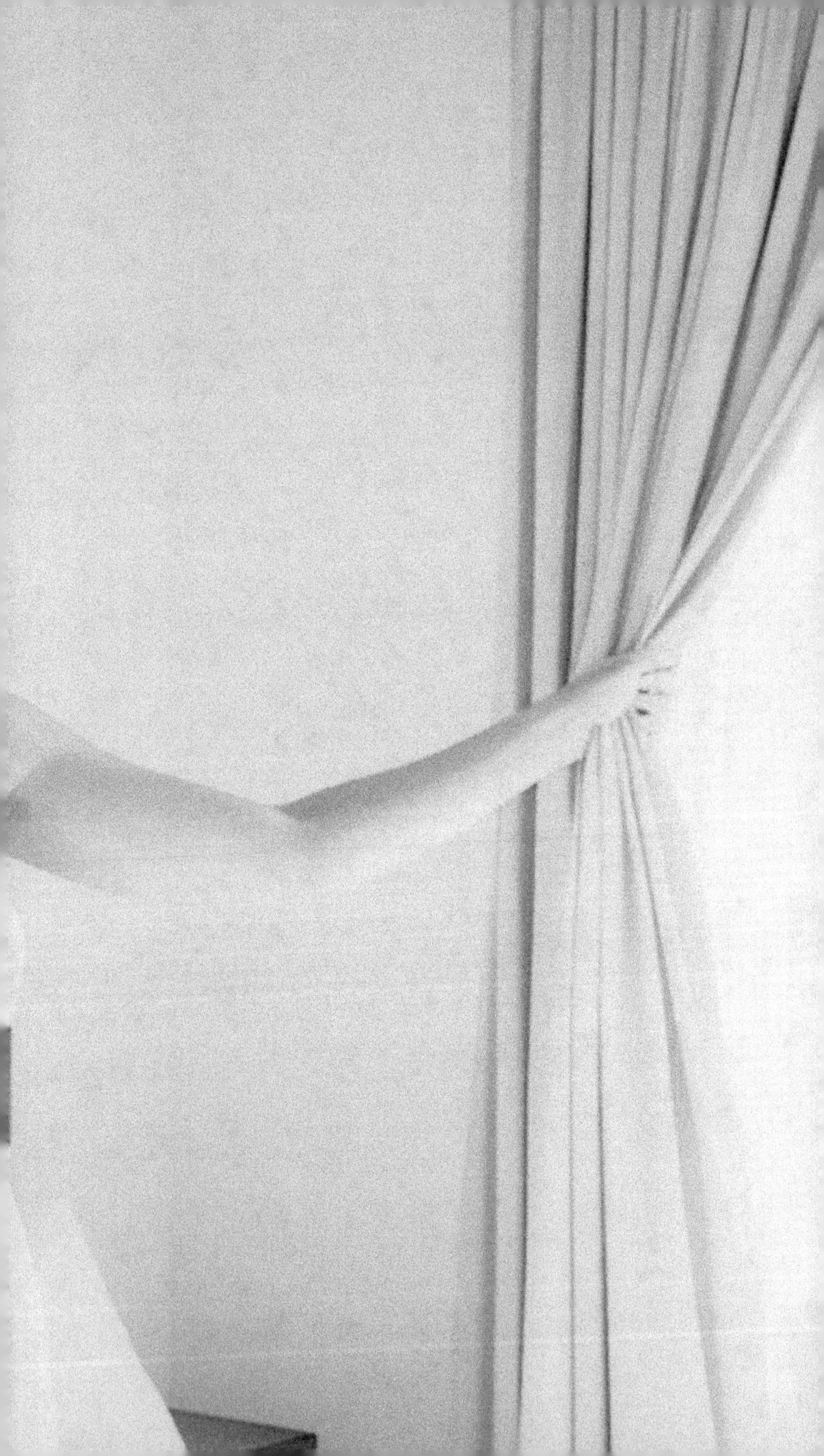

CHAPTER THREE

o Porter stood framed in his bedroom window, just like he used to when we were kids. It was like time hadn't passed. Like I hadn't disappeared. Like we were still seventeen and our lives were still made of cassette tapes and awkward silences that meant more than words.

It was that look. That still, solid way he always held a person's gaze without grabbing for it. It was that look that brought it home. The truth, I mean.

I'd never been in love with my ex-husband.

Maybe I had loved Greg once. Or thought I had. Maybe I'd convinced myself that love was what happened when you stuck around and made yourself useful and kept forgiving the same mistake over and over until you forgot it ever hurt.

This feeling in my chest now? The startled ache? The weightless vertigo of being seen? I'd never had that with Greg.

I'd had it here. With Bo.

I was never loud about it. I wasn't the type. Neither was Bo. He'd sat in the back of the classroom—not because he wasn't smart. Bo was the kind of smart that didn't raise its hand. He just didn't like to cause a fuss. Didn't need the spotlight to prove anything.

I'd always sat in the front. Not because I wanted attention. Because I was terrified of missing something important.

We had balanced each other that way.

I was the girl who barely got invited to anything. He was the boy everyone wanted around. Popularity clung to Bo like sweat on a July afternoon. He didn't ask for it. He didn't even like it. But it came with the territory—starting quarterback, quiet smile, those damn hands that made everything he touched seem steady and whole.

And still, he'd always made time for me. His first friend. His best friend. Sometimes we talked over the backyard fence. Sometimes out on the front porch. Most often we met right here—window to window. We'd talk. Or not. Sometimes we'd just sit, lights off, sharing songs through the breeze. It had been quiet, constant, and so good it made me stupid. I'd crushed on him so hard it cracked my ribs.

And then Billie Davis happened.

Head cheerleader. Prom queen. Everything I wasn't. She didn't slip him mixtapes or learn the chords to his favorite song on guitar like I did. She just showed up in a dress that fit right and said "yes" before I even worked up the nerve to ask "maybe."

My best friend married her and moved away. I told myself it didn't matter. That I was happy for him. That I had other things to do, bigger dreams.

And then I met Greg. He made me feel needed. I mistook that for being chosen.

Bo was looking at me now, like he remembered. Like maybe he'd always known what I'd felt for him. I had the itch to run and hide.

"You're back," he said, voice low but clear across the years and the yard and the moment that had gone too long unspoken.

"You realized I was gone?" I asked, half-surprised.

"You've been gone nearly thirty years, Cellie."

Cellie. Only a handful of people on this earth called me that. My ex-husband had never been one of them. That nickname, more than anything, let me know I was back home.

But I wasn't back. Not truly. I was passing through with an important job to do. A few important jobs to do. I wasn't staying. This man standing across the way from me was the number one reason why I had to complete my tasks and get the hell out of Dodge.

"You left first," I reminded him.

It came out smaller than I meant it. But it was true. He'd left for college, for the future, for Billie. I'd left soon after. There had been no reason for me to stay with him gone.

"Yeah," Bo said. "But I came back."

"What are you doing here?"

He leaned a shoulder against the window frame. "I live here."

"You moved back to Stillwater?"

He nodded. "After my folks retired to Florida. Been back for a while now."

"I didn't know that."

His mouth tilted. It was not quite a smile. "Would it have made a difference?"

I stared at him. Confused. Off balance. "What's that supposed to mean?"

Bo held my gaze. "Would knowing I was here have brought you back sooner?"

Before I could ask—before I could even find my

breath—his phone rang. I watched him hesitate. Look down. Then up again.

"I have to take this."

Bo held up his phone as though it was evidence. I couldn't see the caller ID. He didn't answer immediately. He was waiting. For me to acknowledge the phone? For me to give him permission? Understanding? Like it actually mattered to him that I heard the reason. Since it clearly did, I nodded.

He disappeared from the window. The second his back was turned, I bolted from mine. I didn't even realize I was moving until I was halfway down the stairs.

My hand gripped the banister too tightly. The creak of the wood beneath my feet felt louder than it should have. Like the house knew I was trying to escape and was tattling on me. I moved fast but not fast enough to outpace the thudding in my chest or the ache rising like a tide behind my ribs.

I hit the bottom step and froze.

The house stretched out in front of me, still cleaner than when I'd arrived but no less disordered. There was too much memory packed into these walls. Too much dust I couldn't scrub out. Too much absence disguised as furniture.

And now? Now it felt like a trap.

I'd come here to regroup. To reset. To take a breath. But after one look—one look—from Bo Porter, I was spinning. Heart racing, stomach flipping, nerves flaring like a live wire.

I couldn't stay. I couldn't stay in this house. I couldn't stay in this town.

I'd make a fool of myself. Again. Like I hadn't already done enough of that.

I'd married the wrong man. That was embarrassing enough on its own. But the real humiliation was realizing, twenty-two years too late, that he'd never really chosen me. Not with his whole heart. Not with both feet in.

Greg wanted Kelly. Always had. I was the accidental detour he took too long getting out of. I was the fix. The consequence. The woman he settled with because walking away took more courage than he had.

And Bo? Bo had always been the one I chose. Every day. Every moment. From the first time he leaned out that window and asked if I wanted to borrow his Walkman to the last time he looked at me like I was a girl and not just a ghost in her own life.

Bo hadn't chosen me either. Not when it counted.

I'd told him. Hopped up on too many Molly Ringwald movies, I'd told him how I felt about him. It was in a letter I'd rewritten a hundred times and finally slipped under his front door one night when I knew he'd be out. I thought maybe I'd hear something the next day. A knock. A note. A look.

All I got was silence.

The kind that confirmed everything I feared about myself was true. That what I felt was one-sided. Bo Porter might have been The One for me. But I wasn't for him.

I hadn't been able to look out that window since. Couldn't stand to see the light on in his room and know it didn't mean anything anymore. Couldn't bear the fact that I'd handed someone my heart, and they'd handed it right back, still wrapped.

So I went numb.

Then I went away.

And now, thirty years later, I was right back where I'd started—watching him through glass and feeling like a girl who was never quite enough.

All those old bruises had come roaring back like they'd never faded. Like inadequacy had just been hibernating, waiting for the right season to bloom.

I needed to leave.

Stillwater wasn't safe for me. Not emotionally.

I couldn't fall apart here. Not when there were people still looking at me like I owed them something. Not when Bo knew the truth I'd never been able to forget. And not when I was two breaths away from crying into a throw pillow like I was seventeen again.

But I couldn't leave, not yet.

I still had one thing left to do.

My father.

The man I hadn't been here for when everything began to slip. The man who had always put me first, even when it cost him sleep, or time, or pride. The man I'd put last without meaning to and who now probably didn't remember what that meant.

Visiting him wasn't a choice. It was my duty as his daughter.

I grabbed my keys and bag. The sun had dipped lower in the sky, casting long shadows across the floor.

For a second, I thought I saw Bo step out of the front door of his house. But I turned the corner, and both our houses disappeared. It had to be a trick of the light. Why would he come after me?

CHAPTER FOUR

he Shady Oaks Senior Living Center was
exactly what you'd expect from a place
with a name like Shady Oaks. Soothing earth tones.
Faux wood floors. A water feature near the entrance
that made the whole place smell faintly like mildew
and pennies.

It wasn't a bad place. Just... sanitized. Safe.
Depressingly polite. It was daycare for the elderly.

The reception area had a few armchairs arranged
in an inviting but completely unused semicircle.
There was a table full of puzzle books no one had
touched. A TV on mute scrolled through a nature
documentary while one resident stared straight at it
like he wasn't seeing a thing.

I passed a woman I vaguely recognized as my

middle school English teacher, Ms. Greely, who once accused me of plagiarizing a book report on *The Outsiders* because she didn't believe a teenager could analyze theme. Now she was slumped in a recliner, whispering to her own shoulder.

I kept moving.

The nurse at the front desk looked up as I approached, her face blooming into recognition before I could brace for it.

"Celia Hart?" she said, practically glowing. "I knew it was you. I told Jolene just last week that you'd be back soon."

"Hi." I blinked, scrambling for a name. I ran through the alphabet in my head like it was a Rolodex. All I saw were blank notecards.

The nurse stood and came around the desk. She was in scrubs, a print of little suns and rainbows that did their best to look cheerful in a place that smelled like antiseptic and meatloaf. Her badge read: Lori Jessup, RN.

"Lori," I said because it came back to me now— braces, big eyes, always reading *Tiger Beat* in the cafeteria.

"We were in homeroom together," she said, grinning like that was still something to brag about. "Oh my God, I read your book. The one with the handyman and the bakery owner?"

"*Muffin to Love*," I said automatically.

"I knew that was Bo Porter as the handyman. It was so obvious. And the main character? Totally you. And the mean girl who tries to break them up? Billie Davis. Girl, you totally roasted her."

Kill me now. I swallowed, smile frozen in place. "It's fiction."

"Still," Lori said, dropping her voice, "it's a little harsh, don't you think? Especially with what happened."

My stomach dipped, as did my smile. What happened? What did she know?

"Oh. You didn't know?"

I didn't shake my head no. I didn't nod either. I held perfectly still.

"Billie passed. Last year. Cancer. She went fast. It was awful."

My mouth felt dry. I had not known that. But I nodded slowly.

"She was so beautiful still," Lori added, with the casual cruelty only small-town gossip can manage. "Even when she was sick. Anyway, you staying long?"

Before I could answer, a voice behind me said, "Is

that *the* Celia Hart? You haven't changed a bit. Just gotten more beautiful."

I turned and nearly winced at how good the speaker looked. Micah Ellis. Though now he had letters in front of and behind his name.

Taller than I remembered. Leaner, maybe, though age had filled out his shoulders. His dark hair had grayed at the temples in a way that would've annoyed me if I wasn't too tired to care. Skin still smooth, eyes still sharp. He was one of those men who aged like the cover of a health insurance brochure.

"Hi, Micah," I said. "Or, sorry, Dr. Ellis."

"We're being formal now?" he asked, his smile widening. "We went to Sadie Hawkins together. You can still call me Mic."

Mic waved Lori off with a practiced nod. She left with a knowing smile that would be sure to tell tales in zero minus five minutes to anyone who would listen.

Mic gestured for me to follow him down the hallway. "Let's walk. I'll take you to your dad's room."

"How is he?"

Mic sighed. "Physically? He's fine. Blood pressure's a little high but manageable. Appetite's steady. No major medical concerns."

"And mentally?"

Mic's mouth pressed into a flat line. "He's progressing."

Progressing actually meant declining in Alzheimer's speak.

"Faster than we hoped. Some days he's almost himself. Other days... he's not quite sure where he is."

I nodded, jaw tight.

"He doesn't participate in group activities. Won't go to movie night or trivia or crafts. He won't even let us walk him out into the garden half the time. Says he doesn't belong here."

I looked around at the residents dotting the lounge. One woman was trying to change the channel with a calculator. A man sat in a chair with a blanket over his head. Two others were nodding off in front of *The Price Is Right*.

"He doesn't," I said softly.

Micah gave me a sympathetic look. "I know it's hard to see. But connection helps. Encouragement from family."

Guilt stabbed me right in the gut, then acid spilled into my heart. I was my father's last living relative. His daughter, the one who always swore she'd take care of him, hadn't even been there the day he was moved in. By the time I finished packing up my old life, someone else had already moved his.

"Thanks," I said instead, trying to mean it.

We stopped in front of a door with a simple nameplate: Mr. Charles Hart.

"You and I should catch up sometime. Maybe coffee?" Micah brought a hand to my forearm. His touch was light, not insistent. It asked permission. Didn't make any demands or assumptions.

I looked up at him, his easy smile, the hopeful tilt of his head. I gave him the kind of polite non-answer women have perfected over centuries. Then I slipped into the room before he could say anything else. The door shut behind me with a soft click.

My dad's room was still, the kind of stillness that felt intentional. Like even time was holding its breath. The bed was neatly made, military corners and all. There was a small bookshelf with worn paperbacks, a pair of reading glasses folded on top. A water pitcher on the nightstand. Two framed photos. My parents' wedding photo. Then me, from some book signing I barely remembered, grinning under harsh lighting like I was in on the joke.

There, sitting in the armchair by the window, was

my father. He was staring outside, motionless, as if the world beyond the glass had asked him a question and he hadn't quite figured out the answer. His hands rested in his lap, one tawny palm up, like he'd forgotten to finish a gesture. That hand had once been steady enough to build a bookshelf, to tie my skates, to write out checks with the most elegant penmanship. Now it just... waited. His face was slack, soft with something that looked like sleep but wasn't. Like the lights were on, but no one knew which room to be in.

My heart dropped. He looked... further gone than I'd expected. Not just older. Absent. Like someone had hollowed him out and left only the shape of who he'd been.

I stood there, frozen. The ache in my chest bloomed wide and sharp. I should've come sooner. I should've—

Dad blinked. Then turned his head. Slowly. And looked at me.

For a second, he just stared. I held still, not breathing. Afraid of what came next.

His face softened. His eyes lit in that familiar way, the one I'd always trusted before I ever understood why.

"Well, look at that," he said, his voice warm and

weathered, like sun-bleached wood. "There's my girl."

He opened his arms. I didn't think. I just ran. Like I was six again with skinned knees and he was the only safe place in the world.

I fell into him, his flannel shirt scratchy against my cheek, and for a minute I let it all fall away: the years, the guilt, the distance.

"You didn't need to trouble yourself," he said into my hair. "I know how busy you are. Your work's important."

I pulled back just enough to look at him. "Dad—"

He waved a hand gently, like brushing aside a gnat. "Your mama used to get that same look when she was deep in her stories. You'd think she was staring into space, but her mind was moving faster than a racehorse. Takes more energy than people know, writing does. You're doing more than typing. You're building whole universes and putting them into people's heads. That's no small thing."

I couldn't speak. Couldn't tell him I hadn't written a word in almost a year. Couldn't explain how I'd been running on fumes, barely holding it together while the world I'd built for myself fell apart piece by piece.

Dad reached up and cupped my face with a hand

that was still steady. "I'm so glad you're here, baby girl."

I took a breath, the first one since I'd entered the room. "You look good."

He gave a small shrug. "I eat their pudding and take their pills. That's about the limit of my cooperation."

I looked around the room again, taking in the forced cheer of the curtains, the institutional blandness of it all. "You don't belong here."

His eyes met mine, steady and clear. "No. I don't."

"Good," I said, my voice firming. "Because I'm busting you out."

CHAPTER FIVE

My hands were sweating as I rounded the last corner to our street. Not just clammy—sweating. Jittery and damp, they slicked the steering wheel and made me wish I'd kept a spare paper towel in the glove compartment like the rest of my life wasn't unraveling.

Outside the car window, the streetlamps turned on. When I was a kid, that had been the universal signal. Time to head home. Lana, Tessa, and I would scatter like fireflies the second those amber lights blinked on. Barefoot, breathless, our arms filled with dandelions or our elbows scraped, we'd part ways for the night with promises to get back together in the light of day.

I never minded coming in. Not like some kids

did. Because after dinner, after the dishes and the table cleared, I'd go to my bedroom window. And Bo Porter would be at his.

Sometimes with a flashlight, sometimes with a notebook, sometimes just sitting there with his elbows on the windowsill like he was waiting for the stars, or me, or both.

I pulled into our driveway. Out of habit, I looked up at the Porter house. The second story of the house was dark. One light glowed downstairs, the faint flicker of a television bouncing off the living room walls. It looked like a house half-asleep.

I glanced in the rearview mirror. Dad was still out cold in the back seat. His head lolled against the window. His mouth was slightly open, snoring in that soft wheeze that made my chest hurt and ache in equal measure. I rested my hand on the gearshift, then turned slightly and reached back.

"Dad," I said softly, giving his knee a gentle shake. "We're home."

He didn't wake. Just sighed and settled deeper into the seat.

I stared at him for a long moment. Was I making a mistake?

I mean, technically speaking, I'd just broken him out of supervised care. There hadn't been a formal power of attorney—just a lot of shoulder-shrugged trust from doctors and nurses who knew I was the daughter and figured that counted for something. I hadn't signed a release. I hadn't gotten permission. I'd just… changed my mind.

I was his daughter. It couldn't be kidnapping if your name's on the emergency contact list. Right?

I stepped out of the car as quietly as I could, shutting the door with the kind of care reserved for sneaking out of a boyfriend's house at dawn.

"Celia Hart!"

I yelped and jumped back a full foot. My heart slammed into my throat. Turning, I came face to face with a demon in a white dress.

Mrs. Thelma Denton. Queen of the Side-Eye. Head of every committee since Eisenhower. Her hair was set in a perfect shellacked swirl of white curls. Her lipstick was coral. Her cardigan matched her pearls. She looked like she'd been cut from the pages of a 1957 *Ladies' Home Journal*—if the journal had included chapters on guilt-tripping and town-wide surveillance.

"Ms. Thelma," I said, recovering my breath and minding my manners. "You scared me half to death."

"Nonsense," she said, her smile tight and her posture straighter than my moral compass had been lately. "I saw your car and thought I'd come welcome you home. Imagine my surprise to see your father in the back seat." She leaned slightly to peer through the window. "Charlie always was a handsome man. He's aged well."

I moved slightly to block her view. "He's tired. Long day."

"Oh, I'm sure," she said, voice syrupy sweet. "Taking care of our elders is such a noble sacrifice. You always were such a good girl."

I didn't respond.

Ms. Thelma gave me a look, one of those perfectly polite expressions that makes a grown man want to apologize for things he hasn't done yet. "Speaking of good girls—do you know we're planning the Sesquicentennial Jubilee this year?"

"Isn't that 150 years?"

"Yes," she said, hands folded primly in front of her like she was posing for a statue in the town square.

"Wasn't Stillwater founded 153 years ago?"

"Dates are flexible, dear. Themes are important. We didn't do a proper celebration three years ago, and we need to restore community spirit. After all, your books have brought such... *attention* to our little town. So many tourists these days. You should be proud."

It was not a compliment. I knew better than to react. Ms. Thelma could smell guilt. I was too tired to take that trip.

"You should be on the planning committee," she continued breezily. "With your background and your reputation—"

"I'm not staying long," I interrupted. "I just came home to get some things in order for my dad."

"Nonsense," she said again. "You're exactly who we need. Especially now. It would mean so much to the town. And to me."

I opened my mouth to decline again, firmly this time. Ms. Thelma's eyes flicked to the back seat. Dad stirred, shifting in his sleep. His eyes fluttered open, unfocused.

"Oh, Charlie," she called, far too loudly. "It's so good to see you. Do you remember me?"

Dad blinked, slow and confused. Then, after a beat, nodded. "Thelma Denton," he mumbled. "Your pound cake always tasted like sand."

I nearly choked. I quickly fixed my face, because I knew what was good for me. And what wasn't.

Turning back to me, Ms. Thelma laid a manicured

hand on my arm. "I know Alzheimer's can be so unpredictable. My husband's parents both suffered terribly. They had to be put in homes, of course. It was the only safe option. Legally sound, too."

I stiffened. Only a woman from the South could deliver a threat with a lilting tone.

"I had thought your father had entered care after that unfortunate fire." The smile never left her face.

"He was checking out the facility. We're still making a decision."

"Do think about the committee, dear," she said, all lightness now. "We'd be ever so grateful for your help."

Ms. Thelma walked off, her orthopedic shoes clicking daintily across the pavement like she hadn't just threatened to tattle on me to the state.

I circled around to the back seat and opened the door, trying not to let it creak too loudly. Dad blinked up at me, his face crumpled from sleep. He gave me a crooked little smile like he was ten years old and I was picking him up from nap time.

"Ready to go inside?"

He nodded. Swung his legs out of the car. Tried to stand. And promptly wobbled like a baby deer on ice.

"Whoa—okay—" I caught him under one arm,

but I wasn't as strong as I used to be. Or maybe he was heavier than I remembered. Or maybe life had just made both of us a little more fragile than either of us wanted to admit.

My knees started to buckle under his weight. I was silently calculating the odds of us both going down in a sad heap right here on the gravel.

"Need a hand?"

I looked over my shoulder to find Bo Porter. Of course.

He stepped out of the shadows like something conjured—dark slacks, a navy button-down with the top two buttons undone, sleeves rolled to the elbows. The boy he used to be had forever been in flannels. Bo in a dress shirt was just unfair.

He looked casual. Intentional. Effortless in that maddening way men like him always seemed to pull off. It had to be what he was wearing earlier, but I hadn't seen it. Not really. I'd been too busy looking at his face, at the past I wasn't ready for.

But now? Now I saw it.

He wore his years well. Most of the high school athletes I'd known had traded six-packs for beer bellies and stories that always started with "Back in the day." But not Bo. He was a little softer, sure. No one escapes gravity forever. He still had that chest, that broad, solid, dependable-looking torso. The kind of surface a girl could curl into on cold nights and secretly daydream about curling into again.

I looked away fast but not before the heat crawled up my neck and left behind evidence. Dad swayed again, reminding me I was, in fact, holding up an entire human and not just falling into a fantasy.

Bo stepped in smoothly, slipping an arm around my father's other side. "Hey there, Mr. Hart."

Dad lit up. "Bo Porter," he said, delighted. "I always liked you. Always thought you and my Cellie would make a go of it. What with all the sneaking around you two did when you were kids."

My face went up in flames. "Bo and I never snuck around."

Bo raised an eyebrow, amused.

"We talked. Through our windows. That's not sneaking. You had a girlfriend." I aimed that last explanation at Bo. I hadn't meant for my tone to be accusatory, but here we were. "You were loyal."

Bo didn't say anything. Just gave me that same unreadable look he'd always been good at. The kind that made me feel like he was seeing more than I wanted to show.

Together, we walked Dad to the porch, up the steps—slowly, carefully—and into the house.

Dad kept talking the whole time. "I remember that summer you two would sit in the backyard reading your books to each other over the fence. I'd sit by the window and just listen. You had your own little world. I never worried about the two of you. I knew Bo was a decent young man. And I trusted my girl."

We helped my dad up the stairs, one shaky step at a time, his breath a little more labored than I liked. Bo moved with him gently, like he'd done this before. Like he wasn't afraid of the weight of another person leaning on him. We got Dad into bed, and I knelt to take off his shoes.

"Too bad my Cellie married a toad. I hope she divorces him."

My fingers fumbled with the laces, a knot forming in my throat. "I did, Dad. I'm divorced."

Dad grinned and gave a triumphant little nod. "Well, good. That means my Cellie's a divorcée, and Bo here's a widower. Now you two can get married." He settled back on the pillow like he'd just solved world peace.

I looked up just in time to see Bo's expression

shift into something between surprise and… something else.

I stood slowly, wiping my hands on my thighs like I could brush off the heat crawling up my spine.

"Thanks for your help," I said, not quite meeting Bo's eyes.

He hesitated, like he wanted to stay. Like he wanted to talk. But even if that wasn't my imagination, even if I wasn't making that up—like I had made up so many fantasies about this man—there was nothing I had to say to him.

Like when we were young, he read my mind. He didn't push. Just nodded and turned on his heel. "Anytime, Cellie." He threw those two words over his shoulder.

God help me. That nickname still hit me square in the chest.

CHAPTER SIX

"I have something to tell you, Cellie."

Bo's voice was low. Rough, like it had been scraped against a sharp blade and worn smooth over time. There was a tightness in his features, a barely held tension, like his skin wasn't sure whether to smile or wince. His eyes, those steady, storm-colored eyes, looked brighter than I remembered.

It was the kind of expression a man wore when the truth had lived too long inside him. The kind women saw when they read a romance novel. Or they were dreaming.

This was a recurring dream for me. Bo and I were in my backyard—or something like it. It had that shimmer of a memory reimagined by sleep.

Softer edges, warmer light. Fireflies hovered above the grass even though it wasn't quite night. Unlike all my other dreams of this scene, we were older now. I had lines around my eyes. His hair was silver dusted.

"I've been holding this in for a long time." He stepped closer. "It was always you, Cellie. It was never not you. Even when I was with Billie. Even when I tried to move on. It was never the same."

I didn't breathe. Couldn't.

"You were it," he said. "But I didn't think you felt the same. I didn't want to risk what we had with our friendship. You were always so important to me. I didn't want to lose you if I was wrong."

His words landed like soft punches. They were painful, not because they hurt but because they reached a part of me I'd tried to forget was still alive.

I wanted to speak. To tell him I'd loved him every day from four to forty. That I'd written him into every story I ever told, even when I tried not to. That I'd looked out my window for a month after he stopped looking back.

But I couldn't say any of that. Because the weight of it pressed against my chest like grief and joy had gotten tangled together. And because in the dream, I could only feel.

I felt cracked open and stitched together all at once. Like maybe I hadn't wasted my love after all. Like maybe I hadn't been invisible. Like maybe he had missed me just as much as I'd missed him.

"I should've told you," he said, but there was no anger in it. Only years and years of quiet ache.

My dream Bo reached out. His fingers brushed mine. It was tender, familiar, electric.

He leaned in, and my whole body leaned with him.

The world around us slowed. Fireflies paused mid-glow. The air went thick with everything that had never been said.

His lips hovered above mine, and I finally let myself believe this was real.

That I was wanted.

That he chose me.

Just as his lips touched mine—my phone exploded.

Not literally. Though my body reacted like it had. I jolted upright, heart pounding, hair stuck to my cheek, the sheet twisted around one leg like I'd tried to flee in my sleep.

The screen glowed on the nightstand, blaring the ringtone I'd set for one person and one person only.

I'd set my phone to Do Not Disturb every night

like clockwork. But Zach's number bypassed that. I answered before the second ring.

"Hey, buddy. What's wrong?"

His voice came through choked and breathy. "I didn't get it."

"The job?"

"Yeah," he said. "I'm pretty sure Dad never even made the call."

I closed my eyes. That wasn't news, but it still hurt to hear.

"I overdrew my account again. I bought a sandwich yesterday and didn't check my balance. I thought I had enough for the week, and now I've got like, negative eight dollars and forty-six cents and rent's due in two weeks and—"

"Okay," I said gently but firmly. "Breathe."

"I can't," he gasped. "I feel like there's a weight on my chest. I'm shaking. My arms feel—Mom, I don't know what to do."

I closed my eyes and exhaled long and steady. I'd heard this before. I knew the signs. The child psychologist we'd seen in sixth grade had called it generalized anxiety disorder, like slapping a name on it made it easier to carry.

Zach had refused medication. Said it made him feel like his body wasn't his. So we'd done the work.

Breathing techniques. Visualization. Tactile grounding.

"Okay, listen to me," I said, switching to the voice I'd heard the psychologist use on him. Soft but anchored. The one that told him we were both staying on the ground no matter what.

"Can you feel the phone in your hand?"

"Yes."

"Okay. Good. I want you to press your thumb against it. Just one spot. Feel the edges of it. The temperature. Focus there."

Zach was silent for a beat. Then another.

"Okay," he said, his voice a little steadier.

"Now breathe in through your nose. Four seconds. Ready? One... two... three... four. Hold. Now out through your mouth. Six seconds."

We did that for a few rounds. I kept my own breath slow to anchor his. Kept my voice even. Zach calmed, little by little. His panic didn't vanish. It never did. These exercises helped to shrink it to something that didn't feel like the end of the world.

"You're okay," I said finally. "You're not broken. You're just scared. Scared doesn't last forever."

He sniffled. "I feel dumb."

"You're not dumb," I said. "You're just human."

A few more quiet moments passed between us.

Then I said, "Come visit me. Come see Grandpa. He'd love to have you here."

"I thought you were just going to get the house ready and come back?"

"I changed my mind." Again. "Just come, okay? We'll figure it out."

Zach hesitated. Then whispered, "Okay."

We hung up.

I rubbed my hands over my face, then sat there in the dark for a minute longer. The dream had long since evaporated, but the ache it left in my chest was still fresh.

I got up to check on Dad. His room was empty. Panic hit instantly.

I checked the bathroom, the hallway. Nothing. My pulse spiked as I raced down the stairs, heart hammering, calling his name under my breath like it might conjure him out of the blue instead of with the full weight of alarm.

He wasn't in the kitchen. Not on the couch.

Then I saw it—through the window, just past the back porch.

Dad. In his pajamas. In the backyard. Fixing the fence.

I threw open the door and stepped outside, barefoot and breathless.

"Dad!"

He looked up, squinting in the early morning light. "Morning," he said cheerfully, as if he hadn't just taken ten years off my life. "One of the slats was loose. You know, if you leave these things too long, the whole side will sag."

I nodded, but my legs were still trembling. He looked so normal. Just a man tending a fence. Not a diagnosis. Not a problem. Not a burden.

But the truth throbbed underneath the quiet scene. This wasn't sustainable. I couldn't leave him alone, not even for a minute. I couldn't chase him through yards and nights and medication schedules indefinitely.

We couldn't stay here.

I watched him hammer another nail with shaking but determined hands and knew what I had to do.

The house would have to go on the market.

He'd come back with me. To my condo. My two-bedroom condo with an office I'd clung to like a corner of selfhood. That office would be his now. I'd write at the kitchen table.

Zach would come too. He'd need a place to land if he was unemployed and couldn't cover his rent. The couch would be his until I could help him get steady again.

So much for the empty nest. Apparently, mine came with a revolving door. I swallowed down the lump in my throat and stepped into the yard.

"Careful with that hammer," I said, gently taking it from his hand. "You're not twenty anymore."

"Neither are you."

Touché, old man.

CHAPTER SEVEN

The walls of the realtor's office were lined with smiles. Paper ones, glossy ones, captured and frozen in time. There were young couples, retired pairs, families with sticky-fingered toddlers and Labrador retrievers postured near the blinds. All of them clutching keychains like golden tickets to a better life.

I recognized more than a few of the houses. The McAllister place. The big blue Victorian with the wraparound porch that used to host the best Halloween parties on this side of the state line. Even the ranch-style with the crooked shutters where the Mitchell boys threw that party after prom. I ended up holding someone's hair while they puked in the hedges. A real Kodak memory.

Now those homes belonged to strangers or worse, no one. Sold off by grown children who didn't want to return to a town that time had barely touched, except to speed it toward slow decline. I couldn't blame them. I'd been one of them.

I was staring at a photo of a farmhouse I'd once cut tulips behind, wondering what had happened to the girl who used to bring me warm lemonade, when a voice pulled me out of the past.

"Hi there. Can I help you?"

I turned to find a young woman—twenty-something, probably—dressed in soft cream slacks and a navy blouse that looked like it had never known a wrinkle. Her hair was pulled back in one of those sleek ponytails that only worked if you hadn't already lived a thousand years. She was bright-eyed and polished in the way I remembered trying to be once before coffee replaced ambition and grief rearranged my posture.

"I'm looking to sell my dad's house."

I cringed after I said it, realizing my childhood home would soon be up on that wall with strangers grinning in front of it, holding the key I used to wear on a latch around my neck.

"Then you're in the right place. I'm Belle."

"Like the Disney princess?"

She wrinkled her nose, just like the Disney princess would. But she was shaking her head in denial. "More like the wardrobe. Madame de la Grande Bouche."

"Because… you're a singer?"

Belle laughed, melodic and rich, just like the cartoon bookworm. "Because I like pretty dresses more than I like books."

That got a laugh out of me. I liked her instantly, despite choosing fabric over paper.

"Looks like you've been busy," I said, nodding toward the wall of smiling faces and shiny house keys.

"I went to school for interior design but realized I was good at the whole picture of real estate. I could match tiles with fixtures, but also families with the right home."

"Are you from Stillwater?"

"My parents were. I used to visit summers and remember thinking this place was so boring."

I supposed a lot of her generation would have that thought. When I brought Zach back for visits, he was always ready to flee by the next morning. No Gamestop. Too few fast-food restaurants. My parents hadn't had an Internet connection and no cable television, only public access. To kids raised on screens and streaming and the buzz of constant noise, Stillwater must've felt like a dial tone.

"I moved back a couple years ago to help my dad when my mom's health started slipping. I fixed up my mom's childhood home, sold it, and by the time the paperwork cleared, half the county wanted to list with me. So… I stayed."

I studied Belle. She couldn't have been older than twenty-five, but she had the kind of poise that only came from learning to hold other people's worlds steady.

"I guess Stillwater's charm grew on me. Now I like it here. Most young people don't."

"Because it's stuck in the past," I offered.

"I'm helping change that. Since I've been here, I've joined just about every board and committee Stillwater has to offer. Including the Jubilee planning team."

"Oh, they got to you."

That brought another laugh. Belle had a good laugh—open and unbothered. I envied it.

"Mrs. Denton did rope me in, but I think she regrets that now. I've got opinions."

"That'll do it."

"Stillwater's quirky. Messy. But there's heart here.

I want my kids to grow up somewhere that feels like a community."

I nodded slowly. There was something in the way she said it that made me wish my son had even a shred of her certainty. Hell, I wished I did these days.

"Like I mentioned, I'm looking to sell my dad's place," I told her again.

"Will he be involved in the process?" she asked gently.

I opened my mouth to say yes, but it came out closer to a question with an inflection at the end of the statement, "He will *be*." After I convinced him to give up his life, and the community he knew, to move in with me. But it was better than that assisted living home.

Belle must have seen the turmoil on my face. She didn't press. Just nodded like she understood more than I'd said. "Unless your name is on the deed, I will need his participation."

"I'll bring him in," I added. "Soon."

"Whenever you're ready."

As I turned to leave, something in me settled. I didn't know what kind of woman I'd expected to trust my father's house to, but Belle... she'd do. She had steadiness in her spine and a sparkle in her eye.

The second I stepped outside, I spotted someone

else with an eagle eye. Ms. Thelma, in all her 1950s glory, peered at me from across the street like she could smell noncompliance from a block away. I dipped my head and ducked into the nearest building like a teenager skipping church.

The building was Suny's Diner—with one N, because the man who opened it after the first World War had named it for his sweetheart, not the sun. Her favorite color was pink, so everything in the diner had been pink once. Booths, curtains, sugar dispensers, even the plates. Most of it had faded or been replaced by practical things in less romantic colors, but the bones were still there.

Suny's still had the same checkerboard floor and red vinyl booths with silver trim. Still smelled like fries, grease, and a little bit of time travel. The jukebox near the counter still blinked, though I doubted it had been updated since Nirvana was cool the first time. Suny's was the kind of place where football players used to pile in after Friday night games, jerseys still damp, helmets clunking against booths, ordering milkshakes and chili fries like gods among mortals. The teenage jocks never minded the décor. The food was good, and it was cheap.

I let the nostalgia wash over me for a second too

long—long enough to spot Bo. It wasn't another dream. It was really him.

He was at a corner booth, laughing. Not just a chuckle, either. A full-body, eyes-crinkled kind of laugh. He looked lighter than he had in my bedroom window. Happier than he had been in the hallway last night. Younger, somehow. Until I saw who was across from him.

Tessa.

She was wearing some kind of gauzy blouse that looked like it had been woven from stardust and lavender oil. I froze, caught mid-step. Bo's eyes found mine. The laughter slipped from his face like it had been peeled away. He looked at me like he'd forgotten I existed and now he wasn't sure if I was real.

Tessa turned. Her smile faltered, and for a moment, I thought maybe she'd stand. Maybe she'd wave. Maybe she'd say *Celia, we've missed you.*

She didn't.

I turned to leave, and that's when I slammed right into Lana Russo.

If the expression on Lana's face was a drink, it would've been room-temperature black coffee—no sugar, no cream, and definitely bitter.

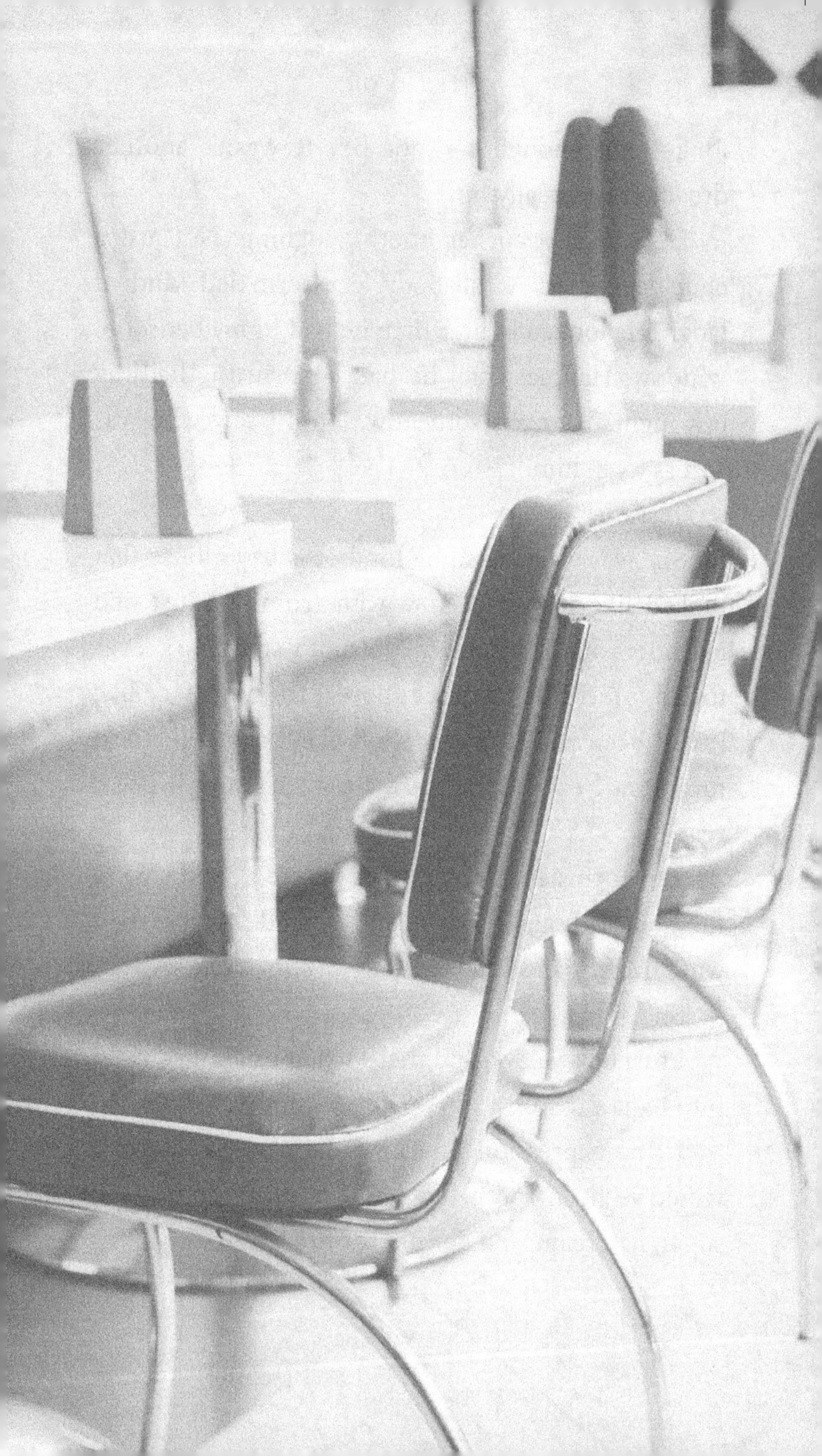

'd ducked into Suny's to avoid Thelma Denton, not to revisit my adolescence. But the universe has a real sense of humor.

"Hi, Lana."

"Celia."

Not even a *hi, hello, how are you doing*? Just my name.

Looks like I wasn't forgiven. Our fight had been so stupid. It had also been twenty years ago. And she still wasn't over it? Childish.

"Celia?" Tessa stood, motioning me over. "Oh my gosh, come sit. It's been too long."

Had it though? Over the years, Tessa would shoot off a text every now and then. Little lifelines tossed into the void. A meme. A memory. A "just thinking of you" that always read more like "just remembered you existed."

I responded. Most times. But I rarely carried the thread. I'd let the conversation drift until the three little bubbles disappeared for good, vanishing like steam. When they did, it only confirmed what I already suspected: I was an afterthought. A nostalgia trip. A pity text in between real friends and real life.

Still, my heart always skipped when her name lit up my phone. Pathetic, maybe. But muscle memory ran deep. And Tessa had once known me before I'd become everyone else's everything.

I should've left the diner. Should've turned on my heel and backed out like the fire alarm had gone off. But my legs didn't get the message. I moved toward her like someone walking into an old photograph, smiling like it didn't ache.

Lana had already moved past me and was seated at the table. She raised a single eyebrow like she'd been expecting a better entrance. Her expression hadn't changed since the last time I'd seen her—judging from the bench like she owned the whole damn table.

I slid into the booth across from Bo and beside Tessa. He didn't say anything, but his eyes stayed on me like he was waiting for the proverbial shoe to drop.

"I heard about your divorce," Tessa said gently. "I'm sorry."

I shrugged. "Don't be. It's not the first time I've been someone's second choice."

Tessa blinked. "What do you mean?"

I looked at Bo. I didn't mean to, but my eyes found his, anyway. "Greg went back to his first love after our son was grown. Guess I was just the scenic detour on the way back to where he always meant to end up."

The silence hit like a pothole. One beat. Two.

Then Lana snorted. "Divorce is just a stage of life now. All the cool kids are doing it."

I turned to her. "Sorry about yours."

She gave me a tight smile. "Don't be. I knew who Myles was. I was the idiot who expected him to change. We can't all have saints like Tessa's dearly departed."

Tessa didn't take the bait. She reached out to me, lightly brushing her fingers against mine. "I'm really glad you're back, Celia."

"I'm not," I said before I could stop myself. "Back, I mean. I just came from the realtor's office. I'm putting the house on the market. Taking my dad back to the city."

More silence. I was starting to forget what small talk felt like.

Bo cleared his throat. "Which realtor?"

"Her name is Belle," I said. "Young woman. Pretty. Smart. We really hit it off. She was—" I stopped.

They were grinning. Bo and Tessa both. Like they were sharing a secret.

Since when did Bo and Tessa share secrets? They barely talked back when we were kids.

But they were having lunch together. They had been laughing together. And now secret looks. Together.

That was my thing with Bo—shared meals, jokes, and secrets. But I wasn't the one who had a thing with him now. It was Tessa. She wasn't even his type. She was a vegan, for God's sake.

Meanwhile, Lana just smirked at me like she was enjoying watching me squirm. Suddenly, I felt ten years old and on the outside of a joke everyone else got.

A waitress appeared at the edge of the table, wiping her hands on her pink apron. It took a second to recognize her. Rita. Same bee-hive hair, same bubblegum lipstick. I used to think she was ancient. Now I realized she was probably barely in her sixties.

"Well, well, look what the cat dragged in. If it isn't Celia Hart." Rita leaned over and gave me a warm pat on the shoulder. "You back for good or just stirring up ghosts?"

I opened my mouth, but she didn't wait for an answer.

"Let me just say, sweetheart, your books? I've had folks stopping in here from all over. That scene in the old quarry with the blanket under the moonlight? Whew! I've made more tips from dreamy-eyed book club ladies ordering milkshakes than I ever did from sweaty teenagers after football games."

Tessa beamed. Lana looked like she'd bitten into a lemon. I did not look at Bo.

"You always did have a way with words," Rita added. "Makes me wish I'd written down a few of my own. Lord knows I've seen enough drama around these booths to fill a trilogy."

I smiled faintly, grateful for the distraction. "Let me know if you do. I believe everyone should write a book."

"Could you imagine? Me writing a book?"

"Just don't ask this one for feedback," Lana said. "Or she'll rip it to shreds."

I opened my mouth to say that I hadn't ripped her story to shreds, but someone else's voice was louder than mine.

Across the diner, a voice called out, "Hey, Hart! Is it true you wrote your books about Bo?"

Heads turned. Of course they did. Stillwater could smell gossip like bacon grease on a griddle.

I looked over and saw Dale Perry—former linebacker and former pain in the ass. He'd aged like an open carton of milk, but the smirk was still the same.

Beside him was Mindy Carlson, one of Billie's old sidekicks. Big hair. Bigger attitude. She leaned forward, eyes glinting.

"I knew that was Bo in the book. And that girlfriend character?" Her lips curled. "Totally Billie. You always did have a flair for drama, Celia."

Tessa stiffened. Bo went still. Lana sipped her Diet Coke like it was popcorn in a glass.

My smile was polite, but my teeth were bared. "What I wrote was fiction."

The diner was silent, but it sounded like a big *Hmmm* to me.

Mindy tsked. "Looks like you're still holding on to that old crush after all these years."

And that was my cue. I had endured enough humiliation for one day.

I stood. Too fast. My thigh caught the edge of the table. "Well. Okay, then." I turned to Tessa. "Didn't mean to interrupt your date."

Tessa blinked, her lips parting. Bo looked up at me sharply but didn't argue. And maybe that hurt more than it should've.

"I'm gonna go," I said, already backing away.

Nobody stopped me.

The bell over the door jingled as I pushed through it. The warm pink of Suny's flickered behind me like a pulse trying to steady itself. I didn't look back.

CHAPTER NINE

The house was quiet when I pulled up. I wasn't sure what I had expected. Smoke? Chaos? A firetruck parked on the lawn?

The air inside was clean. Warm. Smelled faintly of dill pickles and peanut butter.

I eased the door shut behind me and glanced toward the kitchen. Dad sat at the table, happily munching a sandwich, crusts still on. He'd even put a napkin in his lap, though it was already sliding down one knee. No sign of a burner turned on, no flames licking the walls, no pan melting into a lava puddle on the floor.

He looked up, and his face lit up like I'd just come home from prom.

"Hey, Cellie," he said, wiping his mouth. "You hungry? I made the good stuff."

He leaned over and patted the second plate beside him. Another sandwich. Untouched. My chest pinched the way it did when I'd been holding in tears for too long, but then laughed instead.

"You always did make the best peanut butter and pickle sandwiches."

"I'm the only person on the planet that makes peanut butter and pickle sandwiches." He grinned. "When you were little, remember? You made me eat one, and I said it was terrible, but then I stole the rest off your plate."

He chuckled to himself, shaking his head like he still couldn't believe I'd tricked him into liking something weird. Only it hadn't been me who introduced him to peanut butter and pickles. That had been Mom. When she was pregnant with me. She had been the one to trick him. Now it was his mind tricking him.

I felt the truth of that drop into my stomach like a stone in a still pond. I didn't correct him. It wasn't the wrong story, just… one with the names shuffled around. Who cared? The sandwich was made. The stove was off. The house was still standing.

"Were you out with friends?"

"I… was." They just weren't *my* friends anymore. They were all friends with each other. Not with me. And that was my fault.

Dad didn't ask who. Just nodded and took another bite.

We sat in the kind of silence that only exists with people who've known each other since one of them had baby teeth. Dad looked good. Thin but upright. Lucid in that slippery way where hope might have arrived too early.

He didn't belong in that home. Not when he could still make his own lunch. Not when he greeted me with a kiss on the cheek and remembered to make lunch for me too. This could work. We'd make it work.

Maybe we'd have to put those little reminder notes up on the cabinets. *Spices live here. Stove knob turns this way. Cellie is your daughter.*

That wouldn't be so bad. People forgot stuff all the time. He was seventy-eight. If I forgot where I put my phone three times a day, surely he could forget who liked what sandwiches.

I took a breath. I was going to say it—gently, casually, but say it all the same. About selling the house. About coming back to the city with me. He'd need help, and I had room. Sort of.

I opened my mouth. And then the knock came.

Three sharp raps on the door. Not the mailman. Not neighborly. Not good.

Dad kept chewing like he hadn't even heard it.

I stood slowly, my hand on the back of the chair for a moment longer than I needed. Whatever peace had settled in my chest twisted loose again.

"I'll get it," I said. And I walked to the door.

Through the beveled glass, I caught the shape of him first. Tall, straight-backed, perfectly composed. When I opened the door, there he stood, looking like the polished version of the man I might've ended up with if I'd made different choices. Khakis pressed, shirt collar crisp, that easy, white-toothed smile that probably still worked wonders in boardrooms and breakrooms alike.

Micah was handsome—undeniably so. The kind of guy I might've ended up with if Bo Porter hadn't walked into my life and wrecked the grading curve. Micah had played soccer, not football. He'd been student government president, not prom king. Honor roll. Volunteer work. Polished to a shine.

He was the type of man I should've wanted. The type I should've married. But standing there, looking at him now, all I could think was: pale imitation.

He wasn't Bo.

My heart gave a slow thud like it hadn't been expecting company. Like maybe if I didn't open the door all the way, he'd vanish. But he didn't.

"Mic," I said, stepping just far enough onto the porch to block the entrance with my body. I didn't ask him why he was there. I already knew.

His lips were pressed together in that sympathetic, clinical way doctors get when they're about to deliver bad news. Across the street, a pickup pulled into the Porters' driveway.

Bo.

Our eyes locked like magnets and steel. And just like that, I was seventeen again, staring down a hallway full of lockers, hoping he'd turn around and smile at me. His secret friend.

Okay, secret friend might be a bit dramatic. Bo didn't keep our friendship a secret. He just never showcased it either. He never talked to me in school like he did at home. Never smiled at me in the halls like he did from his window.

He didn't smile now. He frowned. But not at me. At Micah.

I turned back to the doctor long after his mouth started moving. I missed the first sentence. Maybe that was for the best.

"—know you took him," Micah said and leaned

casually against the frame like this was a meet-cute instead of a possible wellness check turned arrest.

The lean made me blink. It was a little too relaxed. A little too… TikTok Book Boyfriend Trend.

"Is it a crime to bring my father back to his home?"

"No. It's not. But we both know he needs care, Celia. Care you can't give him."

I didn't answer. Not because he was wrong. Because I didn't want him to be right.

Behind Micah's shoulder, Bo got out of his truck. Slowly. Not lazy slow—deliberate slow. Watching slow. The kind of slow that said *I see everything, and I'm weighing what I'll do about it.*

Bo started walking toward his porch, but his eyes stayed on me the whole time. Just like they used to. Back in high school, when I'd let some boy from two towns over drive me out for pizza and a movie, Bo had always seemed to magically appear. With Billie on his arm, sure, but his eyes would find mine in the crowd. Like he was there to keep an eye on me, even if I wasn't his to keep.

"Alzheimer's is a tricky disease. Some days look better than others. But that doesn't mean your father is better. He could take a turn quickly."

I knew that. I also knew how steady my dad's hands had been as he sliced me another helping of pickle earlier.

"I don't want you to get hurt. Or for Mr. Hart to hurt himself. We just want what's best. Let me help take care of him."

Micah's voice softened as he reached for the doorknob. "Can I come in? We'll talk more."

Bo had stopped at his porch. One hand on the railing, the other curled around a to-go mug from Suny's. His shoulders didn't move, but the weight of him—his attention—was still there, still heavy on me like a coat I hadn't realized I missed wearing.

Did he think Mic and I were… what? Dating?

I'd been back in town five minutes, and already I was the leading lady in a soap opera with two leading men. The dashing doctor and the… I had no idea what Bo did for a living these days.

"No," I said to Micah, my eyes still on Bo. "I don't think that's a good idea."

Micah's easy smile dropped. His eyes flicked toward Bo. He shook his head like I'd disappointed him. "I get it."

"You get what?"

But he just smiled again. A different kind of smile

this time. Dismissive. Knowing. The kind of smile that assumed too much and offered too little.

"You have my number," Micah said. "Call me when things take a turn."

When, not if.

Then he turned and walked back to his car.

I stood in the doorway a long time after his tail-lights blinked out of view. When I finally looked across the fence, Bo was gone. Porch empty. Door shut.

CHAPTER TEN

The scent of turmeric and garlic hit me like a memory. Warm, rich, complicated. Like the girl I used to know, who now ran this place as a boss businesswoman. Meena Chopra had always been the kind of person you wanted to be seated next to in biology and invite to your birthday party. Smart, funny, and disarmingly kind. In high school, she'd been known for three things: her laugh, her debate team trophies, and the tiffin lunches her mom packed that made the cafeteria pizza look like regret.

Now she owned Spice & Sundries, Stillwater's only Indian restaurant, tucked right behind the old train station like a secret too good to share. Her parents had semi-retired, though from the sounds of it, "semi" translated to her father still trying to commandeer the kitchen. I caught sight of him now. His brow furrowed, sleeves rolled, trying to micromanage the naan. Meena gently but firmly nudged him back behind the line like a seasoned general.

Her husband, Raj, hovered nearby with the air of a man who worshipped the ground she walked on but still reminded her to drink water and sit down every now and then. He was currently placing a shawl over her shoulders like the room was 50 degrees instead of a perfectly fine 72.

It made something tug in my chest. Not envy, exactly. Just that low, familiar ache. The one that says: *See? It happens. Just not to you.*

You'd think I'd be bitter by now. But no. Somehow, I still believed in love. The stubborn, slow-blooming kind. The kind that didn't need a chase or a storm. Just two people choosing each other over and over.

Yeah, I believed in love. I just didn't believe that love believed in me. Not anymore. Maybe not ever.

"Celia Hart," Meena said, stepping out from behind the counter like I was someone worth greeting with her whole body. She pulled me into a hug before I could brace myself. "Welcome back."

"Thanks, but I'm not back. Just here to settle some things for my dad."

Meena's hand flew to her chest. "Oh no. I hadn't heard. I'm so sorry, Celia. He was such a good man."

"He still is. He's fine. Not… you know. Gone. I'm planning to sell the house and bring him back to the city with me."

Meena let out a quiet *ah*. It was the kind of sound people made when they're trying to swallow disagreement without choking on it. Her smile was soft but tight around the corners.

"Stillwater was made for men like Charlie Hart. He's one of its bones."

I didn't say anything to that. Mostly because I didn't have anything to say that wouldn't sound defensive or exhausted. Both emotions were always riding shotgun on my shoulders these days.

Meena gave me a look I couldn't quite read. Compassion, maybe? Or pity? Then she pivoted like a pro. "So what can I get you?"

"Chicken curry," I said. "Mild. For my dad."

She nodded and tapped the order into the tablet. I started to say *Make it two*, but my eyes flicked up to the menu board. The chalk letters were different, the prices higher, but nestled halfway down was still my favorite: lamb rogan josh with extra cinnamon and garlic.

The same thing Bo used to order. The one we used to steal bites of off each other's plates.

"Actually, make one chicken curry mild, and one lamb rogan josh. Don't hold back on the spice."

Meena glanced up at me with a half-smile. "Look at you."

I shrugged. "It's been a week."

She laughed, printed the ticket, and slipped it onto the line. "I'm really glad you stopped in. I read your book, by the way. Loved it. It brought in some new customers, too. Tourists mostly, but a few said they came just to see the town that inspired the story."

"I'm so happy to hear that."

"I've always wanted to write one myself, you know."

"You should," I said, more sincerely than I expected. "You'd be good at it."

"I wouldn't even know where to start." Meena tilted her head, studying me. "You ever think of teaching a class?"

I had. What was that old saying? Those who can do. Those who can't teach. I couldn't help but question if I should retire my pen and start teaching these days. On the days I stared at a blinking cursor and wondered if the well had finally dried up. On the days I let the laundry pile up and the words refuse to come. On the days I wasn't sure I had another story in me.

My order was going to take a while, so I settled into one of the chairs near the front, the ones meant for people waiting on takeout, impulse samosas, or divine intervention. I was halfway through reading the curry specials painted on the wall when I heard a voice call out from the kitchen.

"One lamb rogan josh, extra spicy. One tofu curry."

At first, I thought that was my order. But it was too fast. It had barely been five minutes. And I'd ordered chicken, not tofu. There was only one other person I knew who ordered that particular lamb dish that way. I turned my head before I could stop myself.

But it wasn't Bo standing at the counter. It was Tessa.

She looked… caught. Like she hadn't expected to see me either.

I stood up slowly, unsure what to say. Whether to pretend I hadn't noticed or let the awkwardness flood the whole room and drag us both under.

Tessa beat me to it. "Hey," she said, holding the takeout bag like a peace offering.

"Hey," I echoed, voice steady. "Didn't peg you for the double-spicy type."

Her smile was small. Guilty. "It's not for me."

Of course not. But I didn't ask. Instead, I nodded toward the table where my chai was cooling beside the silverware holder.

"I'm waiting for my order. Don't let me keep you."

There was a beat. A long one where she just looked at me. Like she was trying to figure out if this was an ambush or a truce. Her soft features told me she'd made a decision when she nodded to herself.

Tessa sat down next to me like we were still girls and none of the years in between had happened. I didn't look at her. Couldn't, really. Not with that bag sitting in her lap. White plastic, cinched tight, but I could smell it. The cinnamon. The cloves. The memory of a Friday night and Bo's laugh across the table from me.

"I'm sorry," she said softly.

I nodded, still staring at the bag. Like if I looked hard enough, I could rewrite the last twenty years.

"What did I do?" Tessa's voice didn't wobble. It was calm, careful. Like she was afraid of breaking something between us that might already be dust. "To end our friendship, I mean."

I blinked, pulling my gaze from the bag. Then looked up at her. "You have to ask?"

"Yes," she said, not backing down. "Because I don't know. One day you were calling. Then you weren't."

"You mean a few years ago?" I asked, my voice flat. "Is that about when you started dating Bo?"

"What?" Tessa's forehead creased. "I've never dated anyone but Darnell. You know that."

"So you two just started dating?"

"You think Bo Porter and I are dating? You actually think I'd break girl code?"

"I saw you. Laughing. Sharing lunch. Now you're picking up his dinner." I gestured toward the bag. "I know that's his favorite. I was with him the first time he tried it. Actually, no, I had tried it, and he took some off my plate."

"I'm headed to his place. For dinner. Because we're both on the Jubilee committee. Belle roped us in—Lana, too. No one says no to that girl."

"So you're all just hanging out now." I didn't bother to add the *without me*.

But Tessa heard. She had always been an empath. "Why don't you join us?"

I opened my mouth. Closed it again.

She watched me, and her expression changed. Softened. I could see it now: the sad widow behind the bright makeup and melodic voice. The woman I hadn't called. Not once since her husband's death. Shame washed over me.

"I wasn't there for you," I said, my voice barely above a whisper. "When Darnell died, all I sent was a card. Flowers. I didn't even come to hug you. I found out too late, and then…"

Tessa's eyes glistened.

And just like that, she wasn't the woman with the perfect posture and crisp voice, the one who always knew what to say when someone was down. She was the girl I grew up with—the one who cried whenever anyone else did, even strangers. The one who carried Band-Aids in her backpack for wounded animals, who once missed the school bus because she was busy coaxing a moth out of a spider's web. The girl who smelled every single rose in front of the florist's shop, just in case one had a better scent than the others.

She'd always been fragile underneath all that strength. Gentle in a way the world didn't reward. Or deserve. And I hadn't been there.

"You can hug me now," she said.

Tessa's arms wrapped around me like no time had passed at all. All the brittle parts of me cracked clean open. I hadn't been hugged like this in years. Not by someone who meant it. Not by someone who'd known the girl I used to be.

Tessa had been the one grieving, but I was the one who'd collapsed under the weight of it. Of everything. My friend held on anyway.

We stayed like that for I don't know how long. I needed the break. I needed the care and attention. I should've been comforting her, but that wasn't Tessa's way. She just gave and gave and gave. Unlike with me, who went empty from the taking, service filled Tessa up.

"Celia, your order's ready," Meena called out from the counter.

Tessa pulled back, her hand still on my shoulder. She smiled through her tears. "Let's not wait another decade, okay?"

I nodded, breath catching in my throat. "Okay."

I turned toward the counter, but in that moment, I already felt lighter. Like maybe I wasn't so alone after all.

CHAPTER ELEVEN

Tessa and I strolled down Maple Street like no time had passed. The street was cracked and mended in the same spots it had always been. We passed the Johansens' old place. It was now painted a blinding shade of mint green that made us both wince. We fell into a rhythm of gossip and soft laughter, the kind that only comes from remembering people you haven't thought about in decades.

"Did you hear about Julie Henders?" Tessa asked, nudging me with her elbow. "Moved to Florida. Married a guy who breeds exotic parrots."

"Of course she did. She always did like loud things that talked too much."

Tessa snorted. "You should've seen her Christmas

card. They were all wearing matching toucan onesies."

"I'd have questions if they weren't."

We passed the old Miller house. It was empty now, shutters hanging crooked like drunk eyelids. I thought about how many nights I'd driven past it in high school, windows fogged with teenage angst and too much wishing.

"So," Tessa said, tone softening, "how are you really?"

I gave her the answer I gave everyone. The one that sounded stable and well-adjusted and just detached enough to avoid any follow-ups. "I'm fine. I got a great kid out of my marriage and a well-stocked 401K. Greg and I—well, we settled. And we shouldn't have."

Tessa stopped walking. Turned toward me. "That's BS."

"Is it now?" I arched a brow.

"You didn't settle; you survived. There's a difference. But you don't have to keep surviving, Cellie. You deserve an amazing happily ever after. One of the real ones you write about."

"So you've read my books," I asked, trying to defuse the conversation. Unfortunately, Tessa knew me too well. She wasn't having it.

"You've got to believe it first; that you deserve it."

I looked at her, standing there like she hadn't lost her own husband, like she hadn't buried the one man who'd truly seen her , like she still believed in fairy tales. She'd found the love of her life. And now she was alone.

"Are you dating?" I asked because I wasn't sure how else to say *I see you, too.*

Tessa smiled, but it didn't quite reach her eyes. "No. I don't think I'll get married again. I'm happy with my vibrator."

That made me laugh—a real laugh, the kind that cracked open something in my chest.

But then her face shifted, and she glanced away. "I do regret not having kids, though."

"I thought you and Darnell agreed. No kids, just travel and matching robes."

Tessa didn't answer. Not right away. Just nodded slowly and looked at the ground. Her answer, when it came, was so quiet, I knew it wasn't for me. "That was the plan."

Before I could press, she brightened like a switch flipped. "So. I built this retreat center. Wellness and yoga and teas you can't pronounce. It's at the edge of town, tucked into the old Briar Ridge property. You should come sometime. Might even help with that scowl you've been wearing since 1999."

I rolled my eyes. "You offering goat yoga?"

She smirked. "Only if the goat's name is Greg, and we put him out to pasture."

I laughed again, even as something twisted behind my ribs.

"I've been working on a book," she added. "About grief and healing through movement. Breath. All that crunchy stuff. Would you… would you look at what I've got so far?"

That made three. Three people in as many days asking for my help with words. Maybe the universe wasn't subtle. Maybe it was tired of whispering and had taken to smacking me with signs.

"I'd like that," I said, surprising myself with how much I meant it.

We stopped at the edge of the street, caught between my father's dark porch and Bo's white fence line. The space between our houses felt wider somehow.

Tessa bumped my shoulder with hers again. "Why don't you come in?"

"There?" I pointed to Bo's front door.

"Yeah, there. We could really use your help. And I know you want to talk to Bo."

"No, I don't."

"Let me rephrase. You need to talk to Bo."

I wanted to repeat that I didn't. But I also found that I wasn't putting up a fight as Tessa dragged me down the drive.

She knocked on the door. My heart was pounding. I looked back at my house.

"I should probably check on my dad."

"You can check on him in thirty minutes."

The door opened. And there he was.

For a long second, neither of us said anything. We just stared. Bo filled the doorway like a question I didn't want to answer. Same shoulders, same steady eyes, same way of looking at me like I hadn't just spent the last thirty years running in the opposite direction.

Tessa held up the takeout bag like a peace offering. "Dinner delivery."

That broke the moment. Bo stepped aside without a word, and she walked past him like she'd done it a hundred times.

I stayed put. My hand curled around the porch rail, my body angled toward escape.

Bo glanced down at me, then back toward the open door. "You coming in?"

I looked up at him. "Am I invited?"

His gaze didn't waver. Not even a flicker. "Cellie. You've always been welcome in my home."

I stepped inside. It smelled different. No lingering trace of his mom's cucumber melon soap or his dad's aftershave. No more quilted potholders on the walls or dusty bird figurines lining the windowsills. The wallpaper was gone. The woodwork gleamed. The furniture had that rugged, masculine edge—leather and iron and clean lines. It was a man's house now. It was his house.

And there, on the far wall, was the portrait.

Bo and Billie.

Framed like permanence. She was smiling like she'd won. He was looking at her like she'd earned it. It was their wedding photo. I hadn't seen it before. I hadn't come to the wedding. Or the reception. Or her funeral.

Just like with Tessa, I was a sucky friend. Not that Billie and I had ever been friends. But Bo and I were. We had been friends during the first part of our lives.

My lungs went tight. Too tight. I nearly turned right around and walked back out that door. But then the door opened again behind me. Light spilled in. So did a girl.

No—not a girl. A woman. Belle. Bo's face lit up when he turned and saw her.

He reached out and pulled her into a hug. Not a one-armed, distracted greeting. A real hug. Familiar. Affectionate. He pressed his lips to the crease in her brow, like it was the most natural thing in the world.

A forehead kiss.

I'd written about forehead kisses in every damn book. They weren't passion. They were devotion. Steady, quiet, undeniable love. The kind that lingered long after heat faded. The kind that hurt when they were taken away.

Tessa and Bo's shared grin from earlier slammed into me like a memory I hadn't wanted. Of course, they'd smiled when I'd mentioned Belle earlier at the diner. It was because Bo was dating Belle, not Tessa.

I had to run. I had to get out of here. But they were blocking my way.

And then Belle noticed me. "Hey, Celia, right?"

Then her face lit up. She looked back at Bo, eyes wide.

"No way. She's not—Is she *that* Celia?"

Bo didn't nod. He looked at me. His expression was tight, like he didn't want the contents of his past spilled. And I was his dirty little secret.

"I'm so excited to meet you, Celia. My dad has told me so much about you. I feel like I know you already."

CHAPTER TWELVE

*M*r. Porter's armchair had softened over the years. The cushion sagged just enough to cradle the weary. Or maybe it was me who sagged. I sat there, spine curved like a comma who wasn't sure if she was in the right place or not. Belle moved through the room like she was born to lead a charge. She had a clipboard, color-coded tabs, a voice made for theater, and no fear whatsoever of telling grown adults exactly what to do.

"Okay, I want to finalize the schedule by Friday." Belle flipped a pink tab and scanned her notes. "Tessa, I need you on vendor follow-ups. We're still waiting on confirmation from the kettle corn guy, and the alpaca farm keeps ghosting me."

Tessa, lounging on the couch with a glass of

lemonade, saluted. "Got it. Kettle corn and flaky livestock."

"Dad," Belle said, not even looking up as she kept flipping, "you're in charge of setup and teardown. You know which trailer still has the working axle, right?"

Bo grunted in the affirmative.

"Good. And can you rope in Uncle Hank and the boys from the VFW? Bribe them with barbecue if you have to."

Her father gave her a lazy thumbs-up, pride clear in the slope of his smile.

"Lana's handling the silent auction. I need someone to proof the flyers and double-check the QR code links. Last year, half of them sent people to a defunct MySpace page."

Belle's gaze landed on me then. Bright, expectant. "Celia, what about you? What would you like to take on?"

I opened my mouth. Closed it. Reached for my water like it had all the answers at the bottom of the glass. "I could, uh… help pass out programs or something."

"She's being modest," Bo cut in. "Back in the day, Celia practically ran half our school events. If she hadn't organized the senior carnival, we'd still be waiting for the dunk tank to arrive."

"Wait, really? You didn't tell me that one." Belle's eyes lit up, appraising me anew. Or rather, seeing the girl that I used to be all those years ago.

I shrugged. "It was a long time ago."

"Still. We need that kind of energy. And honestly, anyone who can coordinate food trucks, fireworks, and feral children in face paint is a hero in my book. I'll email you the master doc."

Then, with no pause whatsoever, she turned to Tessa again. "Also, please make sure Lana doesn't put her cousin's band on the main stage. We want people to come to the Jubilee, not run screaming into the lake."

And just like that, we were off again—Belle dictating, the rest of us scrambling to keep up. If I squinted, I could almost see her mother in her. Mostly, I saw Bo. Solid. Steady. Always there, even if you didn't ask.

Belle was loud. That was her mother in her. Billie had been loud. She'd been head cheerleader. I wondered if Belle had cheered. She didn't look like the type. But what did I know?

Bo was watching his daughter the way most people watch a sunrise. Quiet reverence. Like he couldn't believe something so bright belonged to him. I was trying to figure out why that hurt.

"Didn't you write a book?"

It took a moment to realize that Belle had directed that question at me.

"I—uh—yes. Fiction. Romance."

"Oh my God, I'd love to read it," Belle said. "What's your pen name? I'll look it up."

Tessa made a sound like she'd choked on her water. Bo cleared his throat. I looked down at the floor and wondered if it would open up and swallow me whole.

"They're probably not your thing," I said quickly. "Heavy on angst. Light on practicality."

Belle laughed. "That's a great hook for your realtor. 'Beloved romance author's childhood home.' It'll drive up the interest for sure."

Bo's head turned sharply. "You're selling the house?"

I met his eyes, trying not to flinch. "Yeah. I'm planning to move my dad in with me back in the city."

He didn't say anything. Just looked at me like I'd kicked a dog. His jaw worked once, like he was grinding something down.

I stood. "Speaking of... I should get back. He's probably waiting on dinner."

Belle was still smiling, unaware that the floor had just dropped out beneath me. "It was so great to finally meet you. And seriously, I'm getting your book tonight."

Tessa gave me a look that said she'd warn Belle first. Or maybe not. Maybe she wanted the chaos. She wanted me and Bo to talk. His daughter reading my revisionist history about him and her mom would certainly be a conversation.

I turned to the door, fumbling for my keys even though I wasn't driving. I clutched the Indian takeout to my chest like the spice could save me.

"I'll walk you out," Bo said.

Not a question. Not a suggestion. I didn't argue.

The air outside was sharp and still. Like it was waiting for me to say something that wouldn't come. The door clicked shut behind us, soft as a sigh. We stood there like ghosts in the threshold, caught between the past and the porch light.

Bo gestured for me to go first. His hand hovered in that same gentlemanly way he'd always had. Polite, practiced, a little irritating because it made a girl wish every guy did this for her.

I took the steps carefully, one at a time, like they

might give out beneath me. Tripping and landing in a heap at his feet felt like the kind of ending this night was barreling toward. Might as well add a sprained ankle to the emotional bruising.

We walked in silence. Our shoes crunched against gravel. The night air was thick with whatever we weren't saying. His presence beside me was steady and warm and... maddening.

"When did it get so awkward between us, Cellie?"

I knew the answer to that one. "When I confessed my feelings for you and you didn't respond."

Bo stopped walking. I didn't. Not right away. When I finally did, I turned to him and saw his hand lift. Then pause. Then rest gently on my shoulder. Just his fingers, but it might as well have been a branding iron. My skin shivered beneath the heat of it. Then he pulled away, like I'd burned him too.

"I responded," he said.

"No, you didn't."

"I did. I wrote back."

"You left with Billie." The words came out harder than I meant. "I left the letter that morning, and you were already gone. Off on your senior trip. With her. I never saw you again."

"No. I got the letter when I got back. But you were gone."

I stared at him. Tried to rewind the memory, play it from another angle, see if maybe I'd missed something. "You got it after?"

Bo nodded.

A beat passed. Then another. That timeline made no sense. How could he have responded to a letter before he received it? And I never got a letter from him.

"Maybe…" I started, hesitating. "Maybe someone… intercepted it."

I didn't say her name. Didn't need to. The thought of Billie curled between us like smoke.

She'd never liked our friendship. Claimed she trusted him, but she didn't trust me. Not that she ever said it directly. Billie was the kind of girl who knew how to wield a smile like a blade and never leave a mark you could point to.

But Bo and Billie had always looked like the happy ending. Quarterback and cheerleader. Tall, dark, and broody meets blond, bright, and beloved. They were the couple on the cover of every paperback I'd later write.

I wrote that letter during one of their breakups. Thought maybe… maybe the way he looked at me meant something. Maybe that night, sitting on the bleachers with our knees touching and his jacket around my shoulders, he felt it too.

But that breakup didn't last. They never did. They were back together before the ink had dried on my letter. And by the time they pulled out for the senior trip, she was tucked under his arm like they'd never been apart.

And I—well. I'd already learned by then how to pack quietly and leave before anyone noticed. I'd gone away that summer, hiding my tail between my legs. By the time I got back, he'd already left for college. I made sure to be scarce over the holidays after that. And then I met Greg.

I looked at Bo now and wondered what might've happened if I'd stayed. Or if he'd come after me.

But he hadn't. And I hadn't. And here we were. Older. Tired. Still walking circles around each other in the dark.

I stared at him, my throat dry, heart thudding behind my ribs like it was trying to break free.

"What did your letter say?"

Bo's jaw ticked. He didn't answer me right away. Just looked at me, long and level, like he was weighing every year we'd lost between us.

"Do you really want to know?" he asked finally. "Or are you just gonna run again?"

I flinched. Not visibly, I hoped. Because the hit landed.

"For the first part of my life, you were the one constant I had. Everyone else changed, left. But not you. And then one day... you were just gone. No goodbye. No explanation. Just a letter and then silence."

He looked up at my father's house. "And now you're ready to leave again."

"That's not fair," I said, but my voice didn't carry. It barely cleared my lips.

"I thought I meant something to you."

"You did," I said, quick and sharp, like it might stop the bleeding. "You do."

"Then why?" he demanded, stepping closer. His voice wasn't gentle anymore. It scraped. "Why did you never give us a chance?"

Us? He had never said that before. Not with any intimacy attached.

My pulse roared in my ears. "Because I thought you and Billie were perfect for each other."

Bo cursed under his breath. Not loud. But vicious. He turned on his heel like he was done—like we were done—and then pivoted back, fury flashing through him like lightning.

"Did you ever consider," he bit out, "that I had some say in what my heart wanted?"

I couldn't speak. Couldn't even breathe. Couldn't fill the silence between us.

He stared at me for a second longer, then shook his head like I'd disappointed him. He turned away from me again and walked away. Each step cut a line through everything I hadn't said.

My feet were rooted to the ground, like if I stayed still long enough, time might rewind and give me a second chance. But time doesn't do favors like that. Footsteps approached from behind, the click of heels too purposeful to be a stranger.

"And here I thought it was just me and Tessa you ditched."

Lana breezed past me, not sparing so much as a glance, and headed up Bo's porch steps like she'd done it a hundred times. Maybe she had. Her hand wrapped around his doorknob like it belonged there, and then she was inside—shutting the door behind her.

Closing me out. Again. And maybe that was fair. Maybe this was where I belonged. On the outside. Looking in.

CHAPTER THIRTEEN

I couldn't sleep. Not that sleep had been a frequent visitor these days. Tonight she didn't even bother knocking. I lay there, tangled in the sheets like a woman caught in a net of her own making. Bo's voice replayed in my head like some old cassette tape I couldn't rewind or erase.

You were the one constant I had.

Why didn't you ever give us a chance?

Did you ever consider I had some say in what my heart wanted?

I stared at the ceiling like it might offer an answer. Instead, it offered only darkness.

My mind slipped back to that day. It was nearing the end of senior year. Spring had been late. In May, it was blooming like a promise no one intended to keep.

It was Lana who told me to do it. She saw the way I looked at Bo when I thought no one was paying attention. Lana, who had always said I was good at hiding everything but terrible at pretending I didn't care.

She'd just gotten back from her date with that college guy who worked at the auto shop. The one she'd had a crush on for ages. She was glowing. Said he'd put his hand up her skirt and given her her first orgasm. Said that having it done with someone else's fingers really shifted a girl's perspective on life.

"If you don't tell him, you'll regret it," she'd told me. "If it's meant to be, it will be. But you've got to give it a chance to be."

I remembered thinking how brave she was. Brave enough to ask for what she wanted out loud. Me? I did what I always did.

I wrote.

I sat at my desk and poured my heart out in ink. Folded every wish I'd ever had into the creases of that letter. I didn't know if Bo would read it and laugh or read it and come find me. But I had to try. For once, I had to do something for myself.

The next morning, I crept over to his house while it was still early and the dew hadn't yet burned off the grass. His mom's car was gone, probably already at church. The porch creaked under my feet like it was warning me. I slid the envelope through the mail slot, anyway.

And then I waited.

All day I waited.

Billie had come to Bo's house, all ponytail and perk. I'd seen her later that afternoon in the yard while I was reading. She walked up like we were girlfriends, like we shared secrets instead of an uneasy truce.

"I just wanted to say goodbye," she said, her smile bright enough to blind. "I heard you're leaving early. That European thing?"

It was a summer abroad program that I'd been thinking of backing out of. I was waiting for Bo's verdict on my letter to make my decision.

"It sounds magical."

I blinked at Billie, still not sure why she was here.

"Bo and I are heading out for the senior trip in an hour. We got back together last night. We upgraded to a king bed. Our parents can't say anything now that we're eighteen. Not that it's stopped us before."

Her voice was low and confidential, like we were close enough for intimate confessions. I hadn't known she and Bo had been intimate. He hadn't told me. But should I have expected him to?

"I'm starting at Franklin University in the fall," she added breezily. "Same as Bo. So I guess we won't see you much since you're going to school on the other side of the country. I guess he already said his goodbyes."

He hadn't. I hadn't seen him, except in passing, for a couple of days. The end of senior year was madness, but I thought we'd have time. I thought he'd at least acknowledge my letter. That he would at least come and say goodbye to me himself.

"Anyway, have a beautiful life, Celia. I really hope you find what you're looking for."

Billie turned and walked away, leaving perfume and devastation in her wake. An hour later, I watched Bo hand Celia into his truck. She leaned out the window and planted a kiss right on his lips. As Bo rounded his truck, he glanced up to my window. I ducked out of sight.

That was the last time I'd gotten a good look at him. Over the next three decades, I barely visited home. When I was home, I kept my bedroom curtains shut and walked the other way when I saw him coming.

We never exchanged another word. I'd tried to bury the memory of that letter. Until last night, when he told me he had gotten it and written me back.

Did you ever consider I had some say in what my heart wanted?

God help me, I hadn't. I'd been so sure of the answer that I never waited for him to speak.

I got out of bed before I could change my mind. My bare feet hit the cool floor. I padded over to the window like some ghost haunting my own life. The street outside was quiet, the kind of stillness that feels like a held breath. I wanted to scream into it.

Instead, I pulled out a pad of paper and a half-dried pack of markers from a drawer. And I did the only thing I've ever known how to do when the ache got too loud. I wrote.

I didn't revise or craft it into something pretty. I just let the words fall out of me, raw and unfiltered, like blood from a wound I'd forgotten was still open.

I'd just taped the papers to the window when I heard it. A crash. A string of curses.

I dropped the tape dispenser and ran.

The master bathroom light was on. My father

was there, hunched and confused, blood on his chin. A razor in his hand.

"Daddy?" My voice cracked when I saw him there on the floor. "What are you doing?"

"I have to get ready. Can't be late for the store. Your granddaddy doesn't like tardiness."

My father had been retired for ten years. The hardware store had been sold five years before that.

I crouched beside him. "Hey. It's okay. Let me help, all right?"

He looked at me, eyes watery and lost. "You're just a little girl. You can't shave me."

I nodded like I believed him. "Then let me get a Band-Aid for you."

He let me. I wiped the blood gently with a warm cloth, my hands trembling. By the time I'd pressed the bandage in place, something in him shifted.

His gaze cleared, just a little. The cloud receded.

He blinked. "Celia?"

"Yeah, Daddy?"

He sagged, and a sigh left him like something holy. "I got confused again."

"I know," I said, brushing his thinning hair back. "But I'm here."

He rested his head against my shoulder.

I held him, blinking back the sting in my eyes. "We're going to get through this."

I wasn't sure if I meant him or me. Maybe both. Maybe neither.

But I said it like I believed it. Because that's what I do. I say I'm fine when I'm not. I say things are fine when they are far from it.

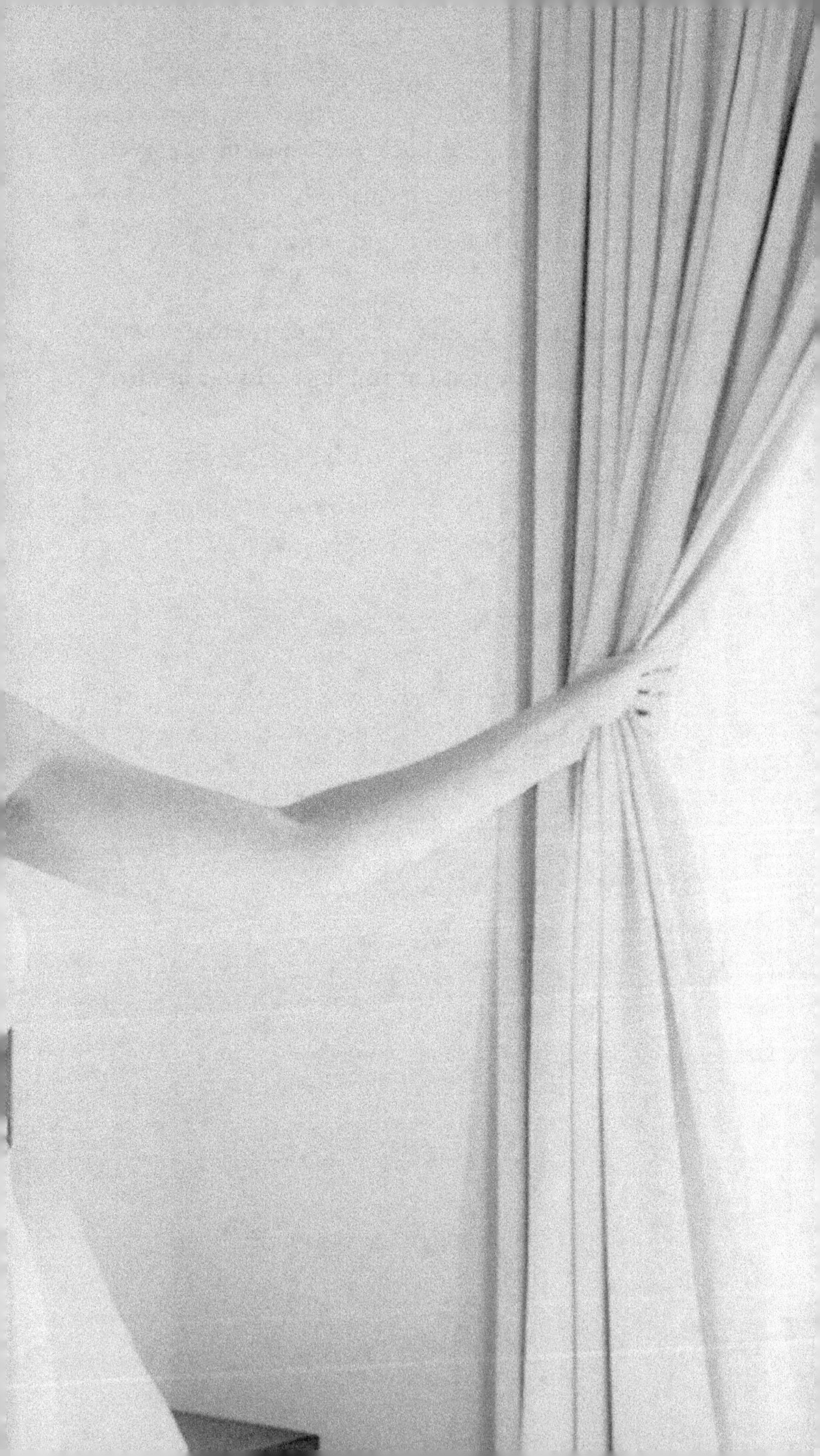

CHAPTER FOURTEEN

I woke with a start. My bones jolted before my brain caught up. My neck screamed in displeasure. My back joined in, a full-body protest of forty-four years and one very bad night in a chair built for decoration, not sleep. The kind of chair old ladies put in corners with a quilt draped over the back, meant to say *cozy* but really just saying *don't sit here.*

I'd sat there, anyway.

My father was still asleep, his breath soft and even. His features in sleep looked like the man I remembered. Not the one who'd tried to shave in the middle of the night because he thought he had to go to work at the store. Just my dad. Peaceful. Whole.

I used to do this with Zach. Watch over him after

a panic attack, when his chest was too tight and his mouth too quiet. Back then, I used to think that kind of caretaking was temporary. Just a season. I didn't realize it was a pattern. A cycle. Something I did on repeat, like a scratched record.

Zach hadn't called in two days. I could've reached out. But I'd learned that no news was good news. My son only called when his life was on fire and he needed me to drag out the hose. Why go courting drama when I could have ten whole minutes of peace?

I stood and stretched, bones popping like bubble wrap. I made my way back to my bedroom, ready to scrape together a few hours of real sleep. The moment I walked into my childhood bedroom, I stopped.

The sun was up. My curtains were wide open. And that's when I saw them.

Taped to the inside of my window, in loopy, hopeful marker was the message I'd written to Bo. On the other side of the glass, standing in his bedroom in a cloud of morning sun, was not Bo.

It was Belle.

With a mug in one hand, Belle lifted her brow. She gave me a slow smile and waved like we were girlfriends sharing a Sunday secret.

My stomach dropped to my toes.

I bolted for the window, nearly tripping over the bed frame, and tried to yank the papers down. It was pointless, really, since the damage was done. I was halfway through tearing down the last page when the doorbell rang.

I was braless. My hair looked like it had hosted a bird fight. I was wearing a T-shirt from a breast cancer 5K I never actually ran and pajama pants so thin they should've been retired in the Obama era. But answering the door was better than facing my teenage crush's daughter right now. Or so I thought.

When I opened the door—because what else was I going to do, pretend I wasn't home?—there stood Bo.

Dark jeans, pale shirt, five o'clock shadow perfectly groomed like he'd rolled out of bed looking like a Hallmark fantasy. He blinked once, twice, and then his eyes dipped low, taking in my very real, very human condition.

"Morning," he said, like he hadn't just caught me in the aftermath of mortification. "Can I come in?"

"Give me a second to change," I mumbled, already backing toward the hallway.

"No," he said softly. Firmly. "Don't change, Cellie."

I inhaled, my traitorous boobs rising up for attention. A feat they were no longer perky enough to pull off. But damn did my girls give it the old college try.

"I want to get to know you exactly as you are. Right now."

His gaze moved over me, slow and reverent—like I was something worth memorizing. All I could think about was the sag of my breasts, the soft swell of my belly, the chipping polish on my toes, and the fact that I wasn't wearing any concealer. The face I gave the world had taken the morning off.

And still, he looked at me like none of it mattered. Maybe it didn't. To him.

"Coffee?" I asked, trying to regain some sort of footing.

"Belle already made me a cup."

My stomach dropped. Belle. Of course. Which meant he'd seen the notes. Or she'd at least told him about them. My words, taped in desperation to the window like love letters for the moon.

I turned away, heat crawling up my neck. "About what I wrote…" I started, voice low.

Behind me, I heard the shift of his steps. Then I felt him. The heat of him, the sheer presence of him at my back.

"Are you apologizing for what you wrote in the books?" he asked. "Or what you wrote on the window?"

I turned, and he was right there—standing over me. He'd been tall as a boy. I'd never caught up with his height. I'd always loved standing next to him and having him tower over me, making me feel small. There were boys taller than Bo, but none of them made me feel that good kind of small that he made me feel.

I could smell his aftershave. I could see the crease near his mouth where laughter used to live. And I could see the mouth itself.

I'd written pages about that mouth. Whole chapters. Years of dreams shaped like his lips.

Bo leaned in. Not touching. Just close enough to unravel me.

"Am I really, Cellie? Am I your heart's choice?"

You are my heart's choice. That's what I'd written on the window.

"Well?" he asked, voice low. "Are you going to be a coward… or a choice?"

My eyes flicked up to his, searching. Wanting. Was that desire in his gaze? Or was I still writing fairy tales in my head?

"You were always my first choice," I whispered. "My only choice."

Bo exhaled, like something inside him had uncoiled. "Why didn't you tell me back then?"

I opened my mouth, fumbling for the answer I should've given him twenty-five years ago.

But he shook his head. "Never mind. I don't care about then." He stepped forward, erasing the space between us. "I choose you now."

And then he kissed me.

I'd been kissed before. By boys fumbling with fast hands in the dark. By men who mistook tongue pressure for passion. Once by a girl in college when I was still trying to figure out where I fit in the world and what kind of softness I might want.

But nothing—not in forty-four years of living— had prepared me for Bo Porter's kiss.

We'd gone to see *The Princess Bride* together when it originally showed in theaters. My mother had taken us to see it. I remembered how Westley and Buttercup's kiss had been described—how there were many kisses in the history of the world, but only five that were truly perfect. The narrating grandfather had told how Westley and Buttercup's kiss had outshone them all.

I remember thinking, even at seven, that I'd

never know a kiss like that. Turns out I'd just been waiting for this one.

Bo didn't crash into me. His lips connected with mine. He kissed me like a man who knew what he wanted and had waited long enough.

His lips met mine like they'd been shaped for the task. Our mouths aligned so easily, so perfectly, it felt less like a decision and more like gravity doing what it was always meant to do. Bo's tongue met mine halfway, like we'd negotiated the terms in another life and were only now cashing in.

We sighed into each other—soft, instinctual, relieved.

It wasn't slow. It wasn't teasing. It was a homecoming.

We drank from each other, pulled at each other, found a rhythm like we'd been dancing to it in our separate hearts all along. My hands fisted in the soft cotton of his shirt; his fingers splayed across my lower back like he was anchoring himself to stay.

Maybe I should've been thinking about consequences or timing or how I probably still had pillow lines on my face. But all I could think was *So this is what it feels like to be chosen.*

CHAPTER FIFTEEN

I was kissing Bo Porter.

Let me say that again, slower. I. Was kissing. Bo freaking Porter.

It was full-bodied, full-hearted, long-overdue. This kiss was the first thing I ever really remember wanting just for myself. My own quiet little wish, whispered into pillows and prayers and, once, the lap of a plastic department store Santa who smelled like peppermint schnapps.

"I want a kiss from Bo Porter," I'd said. I must've been eleven. Maybe twelve. That weird, tender age when your body starts betraying you with blushes and goosebumps, and your heart starts thinking it knows better than your head.

That Christmas, Bo and I had ended up under the

mistletoe at Lana's parents' holiday party. The hanging weed was one of those store-bought ones with the little red bow and the plastic berries. I remember it swinging slightly above our heads as everyone oohed and grinned and leaned in.

Bo turned red as a candy cane, laughed like it was a joke, and then stepped away from the mistletoe and me. My heart had felt like a paper ornament in a rainstorm at the rejection. Though it hadn't exactly been rejection. Because when he'd stepped away, he'd pulled me with him. Out of the danger zone and the prying eyes. We'd gone into the other room and picked up our conversation like that misstep into the spotlight had never happened.

But now—decades later, hair graying, joints protesting, sleep-deprived, and emotionally bank-rupt—I had Bo Porter's mouth on mine.

And it was everything.

Our lips fit like puzzle pieces finally reunited. His hands slid into my hair like they'd always belonged there. I wanted to wrap myself around him. Climb inside him. Curl up under his ribs and live there. But just as I was starting to believe this might not be a dream or a joke or some cruel twist of fate, he pulled away.

"I've always wanted to do that," he said, voice

rough, like the words had been stuck in his throat for decades. "Always wanted to know what it would feel like."

My breath hitched. He couldn't mean that. Couldn't be saying the things I'd only ever dared to feel in secret.

Bo touched my cheek, thumb brushing the corner of my mouth like he was memorizing it. "Every time I hugged you, I was careful. I tried not to let my feelings show. Or linger too long when I had you close. I didn't want to risk losing you. You were the most important person in my life."

My knees buckled, and my heart cracked open, right down the middle. I didn't know how to hold that kind of truth. So I asked the one question that had lived in the back of my heart for years.

"Then why Billie? Why not me?"

Bo let out a breath, like I'd stabbed him and he'd been expecting it. "Because Billie told me she wanted me. She didn't hide her feelings. She was loud and clear. And you… you hid. Then you ran."

I closed my eyes. It was true. I'd written my feelings on paper and called it bravery. Then I'd left. It didn't matter if Billie came between us. Maybe she deserved him more than I did back then. She'd had the courage to go after him and then the cunning to try and keep us apart. I wasn't letting anything get between us now.

That day she'd come over while I waited for Bo to find my letter and then find me. Except he hadn't. She'd found me instead. Coincidence? I think not.

"I won't hide anymore," I promised. "I won't run again."

Bo's eyes searched mine, cautious hope blooming slowly. "Aren't you selling the house? Moving away with your dad?"

"I'm not." The words came before I could think better of them. Maybe it was foolish. Impulsive. Maybe it was the worst decision I'd ever make. But one taste of Bo Porter and I already knew; I needed him like air. Like rest. Like freedom. My addiction had kicked in at full tilt, and I wasn't looking for rehab.

Bo grinned, smug and stupidly handsome. "Guess that means you're canceling with my daughter."

"She was going to get a good commission on this house."

"I own half the company. I'd rather have you than a commission."

Then he kissed me again, like that was a perfectly normal thing to say, that he'd rather have me. I kissed him back, like it hadn't been twenty-six years too late.

We broke apart at the sound of footsteps. My father stood in the doorway, hair tousled, pajama shirt buttoned crooked, and a faint smudge of dried blood on his jaw where he'd peeled the Band-Aid off too early. The nick wasn't deep, but the mark lingered. It would heal like most things do —eventually.

Dad looked from me to Bo and back again. He smiled. "Finally."

Then, without another word, he wandered into the kitchen like it was any old Wednesday morning. Bo and I followed, still caught somewhere between breathless and disbelieving. Dad opened the fridge, poked around until he found the sandwich fixings he wanted, and started assembling them like he hadn't just walked in on a kiss nearly thirty years in the making.

"I always knew it'd be you two," he said, uncapping the mustard. "Takes some people longer to work things out. Lord knows I didn't figure myself out until well into my thirties." He glanced at Bo, then at me. "Billie was a good woman."

I tensed at the mention of her name. I wanted to

disagree. To call her out on my suspicions. But why speak ill of the dead?

"And Greg..." Dad paused, his hands stilled over a slice of bread. "Greg was never good enough for you. You see that now. Had the suspicion you saw it early."

I didn't answer.

"You're ready now. Both of you. To appreciate what you have. To be what the other needs."

Dad slapped the sandwiches closed with a soft squish and passed them across the table without ceremony. Bo and I sat, still dazed.

Bo slid his pickle onto my plate without a word. Just like he always used to. And that did it. My eyes prickled.

My father was lucid. Bo Porter was mine. And he'd just given me his pickle. Life didn't get better than this.

CHAPTER SIXTEEN

was upside down. Literally.

Somewhere between downward dog and whatever contortion Tessa had just sweetly called out as accessible to all levels, I had the sudden and distinct feeling that maybe I was levitating. Or dying. Hard to say. My head throbbed with the pulse of blood rushing south—no, north now—and my hamstrings were filing formal complaints.

Still, I smiled.

It might've been the yoga. Or the steady, soothing rumble of Stillwater Creek just beyond the open windows. Or maybe it was the fact that I'd kissed Bo Porter.

The earth hadn't split open under my feet. It had in fact tilted just right. Like finally, after decades of holding everything and everyone else together, something had realigned for me.

Tessa's voice floated through the warm, incense-tinged air. "Take a deep breath. Root into what you need this day."

I did as I was told. Inhaled. Thought about my dad, who'd managed to dress himself today and tell me my coffee tasted entirely terrible. It was a win.

I thought about Zach, who still hadn't called but had at least acknowledged my *Proof of Life?* text with a thumbs-up emoji. Modern love.

And then Bo. Bo, who'd kissed me like I was the last miracle on earth. Who'd told me I was his choice and slipped me his pickle like we were sixteen again. Who was taking me on a date tonight that I hoped would end in him slipping me his pickle again.

Damn, I was turning into a dirty old woman. And I was giddy about it.

Around me, the class moved like a tide. The twenty-somethings flowed through each pose like their joints had never met resistance, all leggings and luminous skin and the kind of confidence they didn't know was arrogance yet. The thirty-some-things held each shape with focused determination, adjusting sports bras and testing limits they hadn't realized they'd reached.

And then there were us—the forty-somethings. We grinned at each other across our mats with wry amusement and knees that clicked on cue. Our movements weren't graceful, but they were honest. No one was trying to impress anyone. We were here because we'd learned the hard way what happens when we don't show up for ourselves.

A woman across from me winked as she nearly tipped over in Warrior Three. I grinned back. She had soft lines around her mouth and the kind of weary joy in her eyes that made me think she'd seen some things and survived them. My kind of people.

For the first time in a long time, I felt... home. In this room. In this body. In this town that had once broken my heart and now was slowly stitching it back together.

I breathed in again, deeper this time. The creek murmured its approval. My spine creaked. My balance wobbled. But I held the pose.

By the time Tessa had us flat on our backs in Savasana, I was ninety percent sweat and ten percent bliss. Or maybe the other way around. Hard to tell with the way the air clung to my skin and the creek humming like a lullaby outside the open windows. My mat was damp. My spine hurt in three places.

But my mind, for once, wasn't full of to-do lists and regrets.

It was full of breath. Of Bo. Of possibility.

Tessa clapped her hands gently, called us back to the room, and said something kind about how proud she was of us for showing up for our souls. The kind of thing that would've made me roll my eyes ten years ago. Now it made my throat tighten. Apparently, showing up really was half the battle. Or maybe it just felt that way when I'd spent most of my adult life disappearing for everyone else's sake.

I was rolling up my mat when two women wandered over. One I recognized vaguely from the grocery store. The other had the easy glow of someone who'd figured out how to age without apology.

"You're Celia Hart, right?" the first one asked. "The author?"

"Guilty."

The second woman lit up. "I knew it! I've read your book. It wrecked me. In a good way."

"Wrecking people in a good way is my specialty," I said dryly, then softened the words with a smile. "Thank you."

"I've always wanted to write a book," the first

woman said. "Started one in my twenties, but you know... life."

"I used to write poetry," the other added, almost shyly. "Back when I had time to feel things."

Tessa reappeared then, radiant and dewy and not at all like she'd just wrangled a room full of middle-aged women through a series of near-death poses. "Cellie, you should teach a writing workshop here."

"Oh, I don't know about teaching," I said, rubbing a hand over my damp neck. "But I could use some accountability to get back to my own work."

"Well then"—Tessa grinned—"we'll just call it a writing club."

"Yoga and writing?" someone said behind me. "This place is dangerously close to being a cult."

The group laughed, warm and easy. Plans were forming in that way women have of linking arms when it's just us. We'd meet here in a few days, bring notebooks, maybe wine. Suddenly I was being volunteered as the de facto leader.

"Just be prepared to gird your loins for her critique. She holds nothing back."

I didn't have to turn around to know who it was.

Lana wasn't in yoga gear. Not a drop of sweat on her. She was leaning in the doorway like she'd invented enlightenment.

I took a deep breath, remembering the open heart I'd just achieved in the upside down world of yoga poses. "You'd be welcome to join in."

"Sounds like a great use of time. Journaling and healing through adjectives." Lana's voice dripped with the sarcasm that used to make me laugh because it was never aimed at me. It arrowed right to my center and made me wobble.

Tessa, bless her eternally open heart, slipped between us like she was physically defusing a bomb. She rested a hand lightly on my arm, the other on Lana's shoulder.

"Okay," she said, her voice pure sunshine and deep breaths, "this is a judgment-free zone. We leave our egos at the door, remember?"

"I left mine in Savasana," I muttered.

"I keep mine in a carry-on," Lana said with a breezy shrug.

Tessa closed her eyes for a beat, like she was breathing in serenity and exhaling patience. She opened them and looked from one of us to the other. "This is the kind of drama we can explore at the writing club. Can't wait to see everyone here next week."

It was a clear dismissal. The other ladies lingered with the slow precision of people pretending not to eavesdrop. A few offered me sympathetic smiles, the kind reserved for public family squabbles. Eventually, even they gave up the ghost and shuffled out, yoga mats slung over their shoulders.

The door whispered closed behind them. Then Tessa locked it. She turned to face us, arms crossed. Not in a threatening way but in that serene, neutral way only someone who owns a Himalayan salt lamp in every room can manage.

"I didn't come here for drama," Lana said, glancing at the door like she was already halfway through it. "We have lunch plans."

She looked at Tessa, not me.

I turned toward the hooks on the wall, reaching for my bag. "Well then, don't let me get in the way."

"Celia." Tessa's voice was sharper than the incense she usually waved around. "You always do this."

"Do what?"

"You leave," she said. "The second things get uncomfortable, you slip out. You disappear. You walk away from the people who care about you."

My mouth opened. No words came out. What did she want me to say, admit that it hurt that they'd made plans without me? Again.

"I asked Lana to lunch so we could all talk. So

you two could work this out. Because this thing—whatever it is between you—has been festering for years. And I'm sick of pretending it's not there. The three of us were supposed to have each other's backs for always."

Lana let out a scoff, arms folded now too, like we were mirror images. Except she was wearing full makeup, and I still had sweat cooling between my shoulder blades.

"Both of you. Sit. Child's Pose."

We just blinked at her.

"I mean it. You're acting like babies. So sit like children."

I don't know what was more unsettling—Tessa raising her voice or both of us obeying it. But we dropped to the mats without a word. We didn't put our heads to the floor, but we did look up at Tessa, waiting for our scolding.

She didn't start with yelling. She started with silence. That was worse.

Tessa stared at us like we were unruly kids in a sandbox fight. Her usually serene face was replaced by something more no-nonsense than I'd seen in four decades of friendship. Then she sat cross-legged between us, folded her hands in her lap, and sighed.

"I don't know what happened between you," she said evenly. "I've asked. Neither of you will talk about it. So now I'm asking again. Out loud. In the light of day. What the actual hell?"

She looked at me first. "Celia?"

I swallowed. My mouth had gone dry, which was impressive since I'd drunk a liter of cucumber water during a break.

"Lana gave me a story to read. I gave her notes. That's it."

"Those weren't notes," Lana snapped. "They were a character assassination."

"I told you the writing was strong. I just said it needed emotion."

"You said it had no soul," she said, voice tight. "That it read like a deposition."

"I said it needed more soul," I corrected, "because the story was good. But it felt distant. You wrote about betrayal like it was an invoice."

Tessa's eyes bounced between us like she was watching a tennis match no one wanted to referee.

"I worked hard on that story," Lana said, softer now. "I'd never let anyone read anything before. I trusted you."

"And I told you the truth. What? Did you want me to lie?"

Lana opened her mouth. Then shut it. That was not normal. She always had a comeback.

"I didn't know you'd take it like that." My voice caught—just a little, just enough. "You were so sure of yourself. I didn't think my opinion would matter that much."

"It did," Lana said. "You mattered. I mean your opinion? It mattered. At least it used to."

I looked at her, really looked. Past the tailored clothes and the lawyer glare and the sarcastic digs she'd tossed out over her strong shoulders. Lana looked tired. Not bone-deep like me, but close. Like someone who'd run too many marathons in heels and just realized no one was waiting at the finish line.

"I thought you didn't want me in your life anymore," I admitted. "So I stepped back."

"You always step back," Lana said, but there wasn't venom in it now. Just a quiet kind of knowing. "Just like you did with Bo."

"Wait, what?"

"Never mind." Lana started to get to her feet.

"Wait." Tessa finally breathed out and leaned back on her palms like she'd just defused a bomb with a scented candle. "We're getting somewhere."

"I just remembered I have somewhere to be. Raincheck for lunch?"

Tessa hesitated as she sat between me on the floor and Lana on her feet.

I ducked my head, sure she'd pick Lana over me.

"Lunch tomorrow," Tessa said finally. "The three of us."

Lana sighed, but she nodded.

Tessa didn't let her off the hook. "In the meantime, truce?"

Lana nodded again. And so did I. It was a start.

CHAPTER SEVENTEEN

Bo showed up right on time, smelling like soap and cedar and the kind of hope I'd trained myself not to trust. I hadn't worn a dress in months, but I found one that still fit, still zipped, still made me feel like I was worth the effort.

Dad was in the recliner when Bo knocked. It had been a good day. He'd been clear-eyed, lucid, even cracked a joke over dinner that didn't come from 1983. I let myself believe it would hold.

But as I grabbed my purse, he blinked like something had short-circuited behind his eyes.

"You be home by curfew, young lady," he said with that stern dad voice that used to scare the neighbor boys. "And no riding with that Mark Vincent unless his grades have improved."

I'd dated Mark a couple of times back in high school when Bo and Billie announced they were girlfriend and boyfriend. Mark hadn't been the best choice, but I wasn't exactly spoiled for choice back then.

"Is that Bo Porter?" my father called from the recliner.

Bo must have heard his name from the other side of the screen door. He pushed it open and came inside. The light from the hallway fell across Dad's face just right, and for a moment, he looked like himself. All the way himself.

"You're taking my girl out on a date?"

Bo walked up to my father, reached out a hand, and said, "Yes, sir. I am."

"I thought you were dating the Davis girl."

Bo's expression changed. I only saw it because I knew his face so well. "Not anymore, sir. You should know that Celia's always been important to me. I've got nothing but good intentions with your daughter."

Dad gave a small nod, like he was weighing that, sizing Bo up through some old paternal lens that hadn't clouded yet. Then he grinned.

"Well, in that case," he said, clasping Bo's hand, "you kids stay out as late as you want."

For a moment I was torn. My dad's long-term memory was going in and out. But did that mean he was a danger to himself?

"You ready, Cellie?" Bo held out his hand.

I'd been waiting my whole life for this date. For Bo to hold out his hand to me and whisk me away. I turned away from my dad and took Bo's proffered hand. When our fingers entwined, I felt the weight of a hundred what-ifs leave my chest. It felt like for once, I wasn't holding everything alone.

A quarter of an hour later, Bo pulled out my chair for me. The restaurant was new, but it already had that air of old money and curated taste—like someone had read *Architectural Digest* cover to cover and said, 'Yes, I'll take the entire September issue.' The walls were a deep navy, almost black, with wainscoting so polished I could see my face in the wood. Edison bulbs hung from long, knotted cords like fireflies trapped in amber. Every table had a single, low-burning candle and a tiny vase with one perfectly wilted rose—artfully tired, like it had lived a little.

There were velvet booths along the perimeter, the kind that encouraged lingering, whispering, maybe even a little footsie if the wine ran long. The center of the room held smaller tables dressed in white linens and actual silver cutlery. Not stainless, not plated, but the kind of heavy silver that made your wrist ache if you used it too long. The plates were matte black, the food placed like it had graduated top of its class at culinary school.

A jazz trio played near the bar. An upright bass, sax, and keys, soft enough not to compete with conversation, smooth enough to grease it.

I spotted familiar faces tucked into corners. Stillwater's upper crust played dress-up, their laughter a little too loud, their jewelry a little too polished. Half of them probably had no idea what they were eating, but they'd tell everyone in town it was the best thing they'd ever tasted.

"You okay?" Bo asked gently, like I might spook. "Or are you already regretting saying yes to me?"

"No." I shook my head, hugging my arms. "I just hate leaving him alone."

"Your dad?"

"He was good today, but... he's slipping."

"The Alzheimer's?"

"The care home called again. Said he'd be better off with round-the-clock support. But I think Micah Ellis just wanted an excuse to ask me out again."

Bo's mouth twitched.

"He's persistent."

"Charming." Bo's voice was tight.

"Smarmy."

That made him laugh. I felt it like a warmth behind my ribs.

"I told him no," I added, softer. "Told him I wasn't interested in either proposition. I want my dad at home with me. And I'm sitting across from the only man I've ever wanted to date."

Bo looked at me. Really looked. Like he was flipping through pages he thought he'd already read. "What about your ex-husband? You never wanted him?"

"Greg was in love with someone else. I had the misfortune of getting pregnant when we were dating. He did what he thought was right. Married me. Then spent twenty years resenting that choice."

I swallowed hard, the way I always did when I said that out loud. Like it still wasn't quite real, even after the ink dried on the divorce papers.

"I don't regret it," I said. "I got Zach. I got to be a mom. And Greg... well. He ran back to her as soon as she became available. He's happy now. I don't wish him ill."

Damn, I sounded so grown up. I didn't care if Greg was happy or not. I didn't think about him at all.

Bo let out a low whistle and shook his head. "Idiot. What man in his right mind gives you up?"

I stared at him, confused. Because he had. Bo had given me up. He'd never even wanted me.

Why didn't you ever give us a chance?

"Why are you looking at me like that?"

I opened my mouth but didn't get the chance to tell him my thoughts.

"Well, look at you two," came the unmistakable cackle of Darlene Murchison, striding up to our table in four-inch heels and a scent that could burn nose hairs clean off. "Prom king and..." Her eyes landed on me, flicking over my simple black dress like she was sniffing for a brand tag. "The valedictorian."

I actually hadn't been the valedictorian. I'd been the salutatorian. Amy Bostick had beaten me by a single decimal in GPA. But I didn't bother correcting Darlene.

Bo shifted beside me, the muscles in his forearm going tight under his sleeve. I just took a sip of my water and waited for the other shoe to drop. Darlene always had at least three.

"I have to admit, I'm surprised," she said, smiling the kind of smile that never touched her eyes. "Didn't take long, huh, Celia? You swooped right in.

Billie always worried about the two of you being 'just friends.' Looks like she had reason to."

Bo set his fork down. Carefully. "Darlene, the only reason I ever tolerated you was because you were Billie's friend. That tie's gone now. So unless you're here to say something meaningful, keep your mouth shut, because neither of us are interested."

Darlene's eyes widened, hand fluttering to the rhinestones at her throat like they might protect her from being dismissed. "Excuse me?"

"You heard me," he said. "You don't speak for Billie. And you sure as hell don't get to speak about Celia."

Darlene blinked, stunned, but she wasn't the type to leave without landing one last jab. She turned her gaze to me. Her voice dropped an octave. "Just remember, nerd. You don't get to rewrite history. You were always second place. That hasn't changed."

She spun on her heels and stalked off like the entrance to hell was waiting with open arms and a fresh gin and tonic.

I stared after her for a beat, then picked up my glass and drained it. "Well, that was charming. You think she'd be open to a double date with us?"

Bo's jaw was tight, but when he looked at me,

there was something almost apologetic in his eyes. "You okay?"

"I've been called worse. And honestly, she's not wrong. I did want you back then. I just never thought I got to have you."

He stared at me for a long moment. His jaw working. I worried I'd said too much.

"Why didn't you think you got to have me?"

"There was Billie."

"Billie and I started dating junior year. What about before that?"

"What do you mean?"

"Elementary school I get. We were too young. But in middle school, we spent every waking hour together. You were my best friend. I woke up in the morning excited because I'd get to see you. I went to sleep at night thinking about everything we talked about or did together that day."

"I... I didn't know that."

"How could you not know that? How could you not see that I was pretty much obsessed with you?"

"I... But... Billie."

Bo sighed like I'd said something to disappoint him. But how could I have said anything but the reality of it all? He was the golden boy. Billie Davis was the golden girl. Wasn't it obvious?

"The two of you made sense together," I said in my defense.

"Says who? You?"

"It's how all the stories go."

"I liked the stories you told better. But you never wrote me in. Not in real life. Not until that letter. Before that, I thought you just didn't see me that way."

I stared at him, watching as my world reshaped and history rewrote itself. "You... wanted... me?"

"Every damn day of my life."

"You could've said something."

"You know who did say something? Billie. While the two of us were holding our tongues, hoping the other would make the first move—"

"She moved in."

He nodded. "She did. She told me she wanted me. She showed me she—"

"Okay, I get the picture." I held up my hand.

"You know I never looked at porn mags. I would read the stories you wrote instead and masturbated with your words in my head."

I choked. That was the hottest thing any man had ever said to me. Ever.

Bo grinned like he knew what he'd just done to

me. And then he continued. "Then I read your books."

"Those aren't about…"

I couldn't finish the sentence because he knew. He knew my books were about him. He'd read my fantasies. Knew he starred in them. And it looked like I'd been his fantasy, too.

"Me?" I asked.

"Yeah, you," he confirmed.

"Me," I stated.

"Yeah. You."

CHAPTER EIGHTEEN

We stopped by my house first. I told Bo it'd just be a minute, then tried to walk up the porch steps alone. But he didn't let go of my hand, so I stopped pretending I wanted him to.

The front door was unlocked. I'd reminded Dad twice before dinner to lock it. The mom in me remembered nagging Zach to do the same when he was a teen. And even when he was in college, home on breaks. Maybe that particular quirk wasn't an Alzheimer's thing, but more of a guy thing.

Still, the house was fine. Quiet. Lights on in the living room. TV still muttering to itself. A cooking show was on. Dad must've fallen asleep during it because I found him snoring softly in bed, TV remote clutched in his left hand.

He looked peaceful. Not young, not old. Just… still. I covered him with the extra blanket, turned off the TV, and kissed his forehead. He didn't stir. That was either a mercy or a warning sign, but I wasn't going to borrow tomorrow's trouble.

Bo didn't say anything. Just moved through the house with me. He let go of my hand when I went to straighten something or take care of my dad. He grabbed it the moment my fingers were free of their fussing.

I turned off the lights. Checked the door. Made sure everything precious to me was locked up tightly before I went to step into a dream I'd been having since that day in the theater, the summer we watched *The Princess Bride* together.

The grass was damp beneath my bare feet as I crossed the yard. Moonlight caught the silver in Bo's hair. His porch light was on—our own version of the Fire Swamp, maybe. Full of dangers, sure. Unexpected bursts of emotion, rodents of unusual size like doubt, grief, the ache of missed time.

Bo didn't wear a sword or a mask. But he scaled the porch steps like they were the Cliffs of Insanity, a man in black after the princess he'd loved his whole life. Only I'd been the one kidnapped by time, held hostage by duty, kept from my happily ever after by a hundred little sacrifices no one ever saw. But I was choosing now. Him. Me.

We were in no rush as we entered his house. You rush a miracle man, you get rotten miracles. But I didn't need a miracle. Just the man who'd waited.

The door had barely clicked shut before his mouth was on mine. Hands in my hair. My palms on his chest, his back, wherever I could reach.

There wasn't any music. No wine. No nervous chatter or slow flirtation. We weren't that young.

We tumbled onto the couch, me straddling his lap like it was something I'd done a hundred times. Like I hadn't spent most of my life pretending I didn't want this exact thing.

He kissed me like he was trying to memorize my mouth. Like he didn't trust time to give him another shot. His hands slid beneath my blouse, and I gasped, clutching the back of his neck like I could hold us both together.

Bo pulled back, breathing hard. "Maybe we should slow down?"

I looked him straight in the eye. "I have waited all my life to do this. I don't want to slow down."

He smiled. Relief, mischief, heat—all of it. "Thank

God. I was trying to be a gentleman, but I really didn't want to stop."

And then we didn't. He kissed me again, deeper this time, like he meant to rewrite every bad memory I'd ever had.

Between breaths, he said, "I'm clean. I haven't been with anyone since Billie."

That put a damper on things. Billie's name was the wet rag. Then I thought about the words he'd said before mentioning his deceased wife. I leaned back just enough to see his face.

"Wait… no one?"

He shrugged, unapologetic. "What? Did you think I was some kind of hound dog?"

"I thought you were a man with a pulse."

"I'm a man who can't get naked with a woman unless I care about her. And I've only ever loved two women in my life." His thumb skimmed my jaw, steady and certain. "Tonight I finally get to sleep with the other one."

I laughed. It broke out of me before I could stop it. "So I'm the other woman?"

"The other love," he said. "My first love."

I sobered instantly. He meant it. I was Bo Porter's first love.

"Do I need a condom, Cellie?"

My number wasn't big by any means. I still didn't want to give it to him since it was more than one. "I haven't slept with anyone since Greg. Even when we were still married, it was… infrequent."

"That man is an idiot."

"I still have my cycle. And it's unpredictable, so yes. We need protection."

He nodded, taking the talk about my menses in stride like the grown man that he was. "I can't get you pregnant. I had a vasectomy years ago."

I pulled back again, staring at him like he'd just sprouted wings. "You did?"

"Yeah. After Belle was born. The pregnancy had been hard on Billie. We decided we were done, and I figured I'd take the responsibility."

"That might be the sexiest thing I've ever heard."

His grin turned wicked. "Then what are we waiting for?"

His shirt was on the floor in the next second. My blouse had gone somewhere—possibly the ceiling fan. We were kissing like we'd been starving for years and finally found food. My legs wrapped around his hips. His hand tangled in my hair. My mouth grazed the place where his jaw met his throat when—

The front door opened.

"Hey, it's just me. I think I left my organizer in your office."

A voice. A very familiar, very female voice.

We froze.

"Oh my God—OH my God. I'm—I'm not looking!" Belle's voice went high-pitched like she had just seen a scene from a horror movie. She was covering her eyes with her hands as if to block out the movie screen.

Bo scrambled for his shirt. I lunged for the throw blanket and missed.

"I didn't know—I thought you were still at dinner —I'm just—I'll go. I'll just go."

Belle turned in a flurry. The door slammed shut. Silence.

I slowly wrapped the blanket around my shoulders, suddenly aware of every single one of my forty-four years and the fact that I had no idea where my bra had landed.

Bo sat down hard on the edge of the couch, still half-shirtless, one shoe mysteriously missing. We sat there, awkward and flushed and entirely too sober.

He reached for my hand. "I'm sorry."

I gave him a tight, dry smile. "Not your fault. Kids have been ruining the mood since the dawn of time."

But the moment—our moment—was gone. Punctured like a balloon.

I stood up, still wrapped in the throw like a burrito of shame. "I should probably go."

"Don't you dare run, Cellie."

It was the third time someone had accused me of running. "I'm not. I'm not running from you anymore. I want you. I want to be with you."

He relaxed and reached for me. "Then come back here. Let's pick up where we left—"

My phone beeped with my son's alarm.

"It appears that our kids aren't done cock-blocking us."

CHAPTER NINETEEN

till feeling the imprint of Bo's mouth on mine, I eased the front door open as quietly as I could. We'd had one last, lingering kiss before we said goodnight, even though neither of us really wanted to. Still, I'd pulled away. Bo had nodded, understanding in his eyes, his hand slipping reluctantly from mine.

The porch light at my dad's house was on. I hadn't left it that way. As soon as I stepped inside, I heard it. Shouting.

"Get out of my house! You think you can hurt my baby girl and just waltz back in here like nothing happened?"

My heart thudded, heavy and sick. For a moment

—one stretched thin with dread—I thought Greg had come back. But why would he?

He'd already left me—twice. Once in spirit. Then officially, on paper. Greg wasn't the sort of man who circled back. Not even for his son. Even if he had, what did he think would happen? That I'd open the door and fall into his arms?

My heart stopped thudding at that notion. It had never acted erratically for Greg. No fluttering. No tripping. Not even a stutter of nostalgia. My heart had never skipped over Greg. I didn't think it had even been paying attention during our entire marriage. The only time that organ ever perked up during my marriage was during cardio at the gym. Back when I thought the loss of ten pounds might make me feel wanted again. It would also kick into gear whenever I was writing. Most notably the times where I was drafting or revising the hero of my books, who always behaved like, looked like, and sounded like Bo Porter.

So no. It wasn't Greg that my dad was arguing with.

"Grandpa, it's me. It's Zach."

But Dad wasn't hearing his grandson. Or maybe he couldn't. Because whatever year my dad thought it was, I was still married, still miserable, and still letting myself be hurt by Greg.

And Charles Hart was finally mad enough about it to say something. It had usually been my mom who would speak up. My dad would stand beside her. He hadn't had to say a single word. His silence and the disappointment in his eyes had been loud enough.

I rounded the corner and found my father and my son in the living room. The overhead lights were bright as I entered. The television blared static behind them like it was the audience to this dramatic scene. Dad stood in an old robe with one arm raised, pointing at Zach like he was aiming a rifle. His tawny face was puffy, his whole body taut with rage.

"You stay away from my daughter," he barked. "You don't get to break her heart and then come crawling back when your other woman gets tired of you."

"Grandpa, it's me," Zach said again, both hands up, palms out. His voice was calm, but his eyes flicked to mine in relief. "Tell him, Mom."

I moved between them. "Dad, that's not Greg. That's Zach. That's your grandson."

Dad blinked at me, hard. His jaw twitched. "Why are you defending him, Cellie?"

"I'm not."

"You're protecting him." Dad gestured toward Zach, his hand shaking now. "You always do this, baby girl. You always take everyone's crap like it's your burden. Even when they don't deserve it."

I flinched. Not because it was untrue. Because it was my core belief about myself. When had I decided that I didn't deserve things? Like the man of my dreams? Like best friends who wanted me around?

Dad shook his head like he could dislodge the truth. "I told you he wasn't good enough. I told you to leave him. But you never listened. You never—" His breath hitched. "You never choose what's best for you."

My dad's words were cathartic in a way I'd only ever seen in movies and cartoons. When a transparent soul left a body and floated up to the heavens. That's what it felt like in that too bright living room with my loved ones looking at me.

"I'm not proud of you right now, baby girl."

My soul had already vacated my body, but that sentence was the nail in my coffin.

Dad turned before I could respond. Before I could explain. Before I could ask how long he'd been holding that in, and how many years too late it was to finally say it.

At the top of the stairs, his bedroom door slammed shut behind him. I stood there, staring at nothing. His words sat in my chest like stones.

"Mom? You okay?"

I nodded, or tried to. Words forced themselves up through the hardened layers of my throat. "I'm fine."

My son didn't believe me. I could tell by the way his shoulders fell, slow and sad.

"That was not cool," he said. "He needs to be in a home."

I didn't answer. Just stood there in the too-bright room, the static crackling behind me, and wondered when "home" had stopped being a safe place for any of us.

"Come give your mother a hug."

Zach huffed like I was dragging him to a dentist appointment. But he crossed the room anyway, his shoulders slumping forward in that familiar way. Zach had never turned down a hug. Not once. Not since he was old enough to toddle into my arms. Just as long as no one was around to see it, of course.

My ex-husband used to sneer when Zach curled up beside me on the couch. *Mama's boy*, he'd mutter, as if it were a slur. But I'd taken it as a badge of honor. Zach wasn't the kind of kid Greg understood. He hadn't cared about baseball or whatever other sport had Greg shouting at the TV. My baby boy liked fantasy novels with glossy covers and maps in the front. Tabletop games with too many rules. Video games with sprawling kingdoms. He'd rather have been a wizard than a quarterback.

When we pulled apart, I held my son at arm's length and gave him a look. The bags under his eyes were darker than I remembered. His cheeks were a little fuller, his belly softer. I didn't say anything about that. I never did. My mother had always made those little comments. Just observations, she'd call them when I gained a few pounds. I remembered every one of them.

Instead, I said, "You still have your yoga mat from that cruise?"

"Yeah. Why?"

"You always liked yoga. There's a studio in town that my friend runs. Might be nice to stretch a little."

Zach shrugged, which in his language meant *maybe*. He followed me into the kitchen while I put the kettle on and pulled out the chamomile. I stirred honey into both mugs and handed him one. He sank onto one of the island high chairs like a sad prince unhappy with his throne.

"It's not working," he said.

"What isn't?"

"The job hunt." He stared into his mug like the answers might float to the surface. "I'm doing everything I'm supposed to. Applications. Emails. Following up. And it's like I don't exist. No callbacks. Nothing."

I sat beside him. "That's frustrating."

"It's more than frustrating," he snapped, then caught himself and softened. "Sorry. Just… the least they could do is say no. You know? Ghosting is worse."

I took a slow sip of tea to keep from speaking too soon. Every fiber of me wanted to pick up the phone, call a few HR departments, demand someone look at my baby's résumé. But I'd done too much of that already. And it hadn't helped.

"You've done your part," I said instead. "So what's the plan now?"

He shrugged again. "I'm gonna stay here a couple days. Clear my head. Then get back to it."

I nodded like that was fine. Like I wasn't already doing the math on groceries and utilities and how many days "a couple" would stretch into this time.

Like I didn't see the way he already seemed to be exhaling, easing into the assumption that he could rest here. Because I'd keep things together.

I always did.

Zach sipped his tea, eyes already half-lidded, his body sinking deeper into the high chair.

I just sat there, letting the silence fill the space between us. Letting him rest. Even though I couldn't.

CHAPTER TWENTY

The dream clung to me like the weight of warm sheets on a cold morning. Bo's hands, my skin, the way his mouth moved like it knew secrets I'd forgotten I kept. We were alone in his living room, no interruptions, no apologies, just heat and history and that terrible, wonderful ache of being wanted. Really wanted. The kind that makes your breath catch and your knees untrustworthy.

And then the sun elbowed its way through the curtains, prying my eyelids apart and chasing the last of that dream into the shadows.

I groaned as my traitorous body tugged me awake. The pastel wallpaper of my childhood room was peeling in one corner, right above where I used to tape my *Teen Beat* posters. I sat up, disoriented for a moment, the dream and memory tangling.

I turned toward the window, more habit than hope. But there it was—the window across the yard. Bo's. And taped to the inside of the glass was a single sheet of printer paper. On it, bold and unmistakable, was the letter T.

I didn't even need the rest of the letters. Grinning like an idiot, I tossed off the blanket and started yanking on clothes. My hand went straight for the cleanest T-shirt I could find and jeans that didn't have elastic in the waistband. I finger-combed my hair, swished some mouthwash around my teeth like it was doing the work of a shower, and called it good enough.

Downstairs, the television was still on, playing some late-night cartoon rerun at a low volume. Zach was on the couch, mouth open, one sock on, snacks scattered like confetti on the coffee table. I paused for a second. The maternal urge to clean around him pulsed strong. But no. No. I'd done that show before.

But I also didn't want to wake my son up to deal with him. He was not a morning person. I'd deal with him when I came back in from my rendezvous with my…

What was Bo to me?

I couldn't call him my lover. At least not yet.

Was he my boyfriend? We'd only been on one date.

I couldn't say partner, could I? Again, just one date.

But he was mine. And I was his. That was as much definition as I needed. I had no idea what we'd say to other people. I didn't really care what they thought. I only cared what he thought.

The screen door creaked as I stepped into the backyard. The cool morning air wrapped around me like a promise I wasn't sure I deserved.

Nope. Scratch that. I did deserve this. I deserved this bit of happiness. I might not have worked for it, but I sure as hell had suffered enough for it.

Bo was already there, leaning against the fence like some kind of small-town James Bond. His suit was navy, sharp enough to cut glass, with a white shirt underneath that made his skin look sun-kissed. The gray hairs at his temples sparkled under the early morning sun in a way that made my breath catch. No tie. Top button undone. Like he had some-where important to be but didn't mind being a little undone for me.

He had a mug in each hand. He sipped from one. When he saw me, he offered the other with a smile that made my stomach flip in a way no dream ever could.

"Good morning," he said.

And damn if it wasn't. I took the mug from him. My fingers brushed his just long enough to make the heat of the ceramic feel secondary.

Mint. Of course it was. It was my favorite.

Bo had always remembered that. Sunday mornings in the backyard, his flannel shirt sleeves rolled to his elbows, the sports section of the newspaper folded beside him, and that mug waiting for me like it belonged in my hand. If he'd gone to church, he'd swing by the café and get the good stuff. If not, he'd make it himself: crushed leaves from the little pot by the porch that I'd teased him about babying like a bonsai.

Back then, I told myself it was just him being neighborly. Now I could see it for what it was. The way he remembered things no one else bothered to. The way he sat with me like my company wasn't an obligation but a quiet privilege.

He was always attentive. Gentle. Steady.

The kind of boy who made you tea the way you liked it.

The kind of man you didn't believe would ever want you.

That wasn't his fault. That was me. All of me. Too many years of being needed but never chosen had rewired something inside me.

I took the mug in one hand. With the other, I reached behind his neck and pulled him down to me. He didn't resist. His lips were warm, familiar in a way that made my stomach tighten. But there was still that thrill—that pulse of want, thick and unmistakable.

Bo Porter tasted like Earl Grey. Sharp and smoky, with that hit of bergamot that always reminded me of citrus rinds. I'd never been a fan. Too perfumed. Too insistent. Mint slipped in softly and sat with you. Earl Grey demanded attention. I ignored the taste of the leaves and drank him down instead.

We kissed like we'd started something we had no intention of stopping. Bo's hand curved against my lower back, grounding me. I kissed him like I remembered every second of the dream I'd had. I kissed him like that dream was now my reality.

When we finally pulled apart, I was breathing a little harder. So was he.

"Good morning," I murmured against his lips, the words settling low in my throat.

"Damn if it isn't," he said.

I took a sip of the mint, washing down the taste of bergamot and Bo. It was my new favorite combination.

"Everything go okay last night?"

I hesitated. It was a reflex. Years of trained muscle memory, of smiling and nodding and carrying on because who wants to hear about the mess? Definitely not Greg, who'd tune out the second the conversation veered into anything that couldn't be fixed with a check or a half-hearted apology.

Zach tried. But his attention would scatter—pulled toward his phone, his game, whatever buzzing distraction waited to save him from the weight of his mother's worries. And I never told him much, anyway. He was my son. Not my sounding board.

Tessa and Lana would've listened once. But our friendship had been fractured for too long. The rhythm we had was out of sync now, like trying to dance to a song you couldn't quite remember.

And Dad… well, Dad had always listened. But the man who knew how to sit in silence and hear every word I didn't say was more memory than present.

Bo didn't move as he waited for me to fill the

silence. He didn't press me for words. He just watched me like he had all the time in the world.

"Talk to me," he said, soft but steady.

His words didn't register at first. Not because I didn't understand them. But because no one had said them to me in... I couldn't remember when. Maybe ever. So I gave him a little.

"Dad had an episode when I got home last night," I said, my voice low. "He thought Zach was Greg."

Bo's face didn't shift with pity or awkwardness. He just nodded like he was with me, like I wasn't unloading but simply offering him a part of me.

"He yelled at him. Got real worked up. Told me I always take everybody's crap. That he was disappointed in me." I swallowed. "And then he stormed off to bed."

Bo didn't tell me it was okay, or that Dad didn't mean it. He just listened. That was all. And it was everything.

"I'm worried it's going to get worse. That I won't be able to handle it when it does."

Still, he didn't say a word. Not right away. Just kept his eyes on mine, staring into them like they mattered more than anything else around us. Like I mattered.

I looked down into my mug, watching the steam

curl up like a slow exhale. "Do you think I should take him back to the care facility?"

Bo reached out and set his tea down on the fencepost. Then he turned to me, slow and sure. "I don't know," he said. "But whatever you decide… I'll support it. Every step of the way."

It shouldn't have undone me the way it did. But it did. I wrapped my arms around his waist, leaned into the warmth of him, and tilted my head back.

He didn't make me wait. He just kissed me. The kind of kiss that wasn't a promise or an escape but a balm. Like he saw the cracks and kissed them, anyway. Like maybe, just maybe, I didn't have to be whole to be held.

"I am so sorry to interrupt you guys again."

I looked up to find Belle grinning at us. But it wasn't her face I saw. It was her mother's.

CHAPTER TWENTY-ONE

"*D*ad, you're gonna be late to the showing."

The second I saw Belle, I let go of Bo. It wasn't rational. But her face—God, her face—I saw it now.

It wasn't just that she had Billie's cheekbones or Billie's confident stride or Billie's knack for commanding a room before she even opened her mouth. It was that, for one long, dumb second, I thought she was Billie. And that old familiar sinking feeling bloomed in my gut like clockwork.

Of course, Bo would choose Billie. They made sense. He was the jock, and she was the cheerleader, and I was…

No, stop. That was the kind of thinking that kept us apart for decades when we could have been together. I wasn't seventeen anymore. We weren't in high school. And Billie wasn't here. This wasn't her love story.

It was mine.

Bo looked down at me like I was the only thing tethering him to the earth. He leaned in, soft and sure, and pressed one more kiss to my lips. "Can I see you tonight?"

I swallowed, my throat suddenly thick with all the ways I'd been second place. I nodded anyway.

"This time, no interruptions," he added, throwing a look at Belle and wagging a playful finger in her direction.

She held up her hands and grinned. "Message received."

And then he was gone, suit coat catching the breeze like he'd stepped out of a dream and into his real life, leaving me with his daughter—and a whole heap of insecurities I hadn't invited to this party.

"I really am sorry about last night," Belle said. "I knew you two were out; I just didn't think you'd be back so soon. I only stopped by to grab something I'd left behind."

I nodded, hoping the bobbing motion would help me swallow down my lingering doubts. "No harm done."

"I swear I'm not always at his place. We've just kind of taken over while we plan the Jubilee. My condo's a shoebox."

I managed a smile back, but my grip on the mug in my hand had tightened. My knuckles ached from the pressure.

"I'll make sure to call first next time," Belle added. "Now that my dad has a girlfriend and all."

That word—*girlfriend*—hit me like a cymbal crash. Had Bo called me that? In front of his daughter?

I cleared my throat and asked the question burning through the crap in my throat. "Do you... *mind?*"

Belle frowned, then caught on. "Oh. No. Not at all. Honestly, I'm glad he has someone in his life. He hasn't been happy since Mom died. These last few days? With you back in his life? He's been... lighter."

Her fingers wrapped around mine. "I just want him to be happy."

Bo hadn't been happy since Billie died. Because she was the love of his life. The woman he'd built a family with. The one he lost too soon.

I should've felt honored to be let in now, to be seen. Instead, all I could feel was the echo of a door I hadn't even known I'd closed. A quiet whisper in my chest wondering if maybe I wasn't stepping into a love story at all—just a shadow of someone else's happy ending.

The back door creaked open behind me.

"Hey, is there any"—Zach's voice broke the morning stillness, followed by the shuffle of bare feet on the porch—"breakfast?"

Zach's gaze homed in on Belle. She stood at the edge of the lawn, one hand tucked into her blazer pocket, the other holding her phone like she might take a call at any second. She looked up when Zach appeared and smiled, sunshine-bright and confident, like she was well aware of the effect she had on people.

And sure enough, I saw it hit him. That look.

I'd worn it once, at thirteen, standing across from Bo Porter in the gymnasium-turned-dance-hall with a corsage strangling my wrist and hope blooming like a rash under my skin. I'd recognize that look anywhere. That dumb, awe-struck, what-just-happened-to-my-heart expression. Zach had just been struck by lightning. And its name was Belle.

Belle gave a little wave. "Hi! I'm Belle."

Zach blinked, mouth parting like someone had stolen all the vowels from his vocabulary. "I—I—uh, hi. I'm—um. Zach."

I didn't need to be a fortune teller to see where this train was headed. Belle's grin widened, and bless her, she didn't laugh at his fumbling. She just tucked her phone away and took a step forward. All perfect manners like her mother.

"Nice to meet you, Zach," she said, extending a hand with the easy confidence of someone who'd never once questioned whether they belonged. "I'm Bo's daughter. Our parents were neighbors growing up."

"Oh. Cool. You, uh… Do you live here?"

Belle laughed, a sharp little burst that rubbed the hairs on the back of my neck the wrong way. "God, no. Can you imagine still living with your parents at our age?"

Zach's ears turned pink.

Belle paused, the smile slipping just enough to show that she'd registered it. "Not that there's anything wrong with that. I mean—I totally did. For a few months after college, until I figured out what the hell I was doing."

She tucked her hair behind one ear, a flicker of self-awareness smoothing the edge of her voice. "I run my grandfather's real estate business now. So technically, I'm a nepo baby."

Zach gave a short, uncertain laugh. "That's cool. Uh… I'm sort of… between jobs."

Belle nodded, her smile tightening just a touch. "I've been there."

"I'm not a writer like my mom. I do art. Drawings."

"That's so cool. I'd love to see your work."

Zach nodded.

Silence bloomed between them. Not heavy but definitely awkward. It was like someone watching their kid try to ride a bike down a gravel hill, waiting for them to fall and skin their knee.

Zach scratched the back of his neck. "Well, uh. It was nice to meet you."

Belle smiled again, gentler this time. "You too."

Neither of them moved. So I did what I always did. I stepped in and broke the moment before anyone could get hurt. Or hope.

"It was good seeing you again, Belle."

Belle glanced back at me, nodded, then gave Zach one last little wave before turning to leave. "I'll see you at the Jubilee meeting tonight."

I made a noncommittal sound, then grabbed Zach's arm. Not hard, just firmly. I steered him back toward the house before he could embarrass himself further. Or worse, before he got ideas. Dangerous, hopeful, heart-splintering ideas.

"So what have you got planned today, buddy?"

"I don't know. I just woke up."

"Hey, have you thought about looking for jobs here? Local stuff, something stable?"

Zach's brow wrinkled. "What? I just got here, Mom. I thought I could breathe for like two seconds. I'm gonna take a shower and change."

And just like that, he was gone. Up the stairs with no breakfast and no plan.

I stared after him for a long moment before sighing and turning back toward the kitchen. I hadn't meant to come down so hard on him. But he didn't have any armor. And girls like Belle didn't wait around for boys still figuring out how to lace theirs up.

Zach was mine to protect. I just didn't know how to do it without breaking something else in the process.

CHAPTER TWENTY-TWO

I got some words down today. Not many, but more than zero. These days, that counted as a win. Half a page of dialogue where no one asked the heroine for anything, no one needed saving, and no one forgot her name. Fiction was good like that.

Back in the real world, Dad was quiet most of the day. Not asleep. Not exactly awake either. He sat in front of the television, the glow flickering against his face like firelight, his gaze fixed somewhere past the screen. Not watching. Just… sitting. Breathing.

It reminded me of the common room at the care facility—the way the residents stared into space while the nurses adjusted pillows and the thermostat. I'd hated that room. I'd hated that it felt like a waiting room for the end of things.

I cleared my throat and asked him if he wanted to go for a walk. The sun was warm, and the breeze wasn't biting. He shook his head. Didn't look at me. But the head shake was something. At least he'd acknowledged me.

Zach stayed holed up in the guest room, the muffled sounds of monsters and gunfire leaking under the door. I didn't knock. Didn't ask what level he was on or if he'd applied to the list of jobs I'd emailed him last night. I told myself it wasn't worth a fight. Told myself I was trying something new—something called boundaries.

Didn't change the urge to slide a few job postings under the door. Or call the community college about its hiring board. Or look up internships with benefits. Instead, I maintained the boundary I'd set for myself and gathered my bag and keys and told Dad I'd be back soon. He didn't respond.

Twenty minutes later, I was parked on Main Street. Stillwater Spring's Town Hall was a squat, stubborn little building made of brick. It had once been a post office, then a schoolhouse, then an event space before settling into its current role as the heart of civic life. The floors creaked like a haunted house, and the windows never quite latched shut, but no one minded. We weren't fancy here. Just loud and loyal and nosy.

Inside, it was already packed. The folding chairs were pulled out in uneven rows; the air buzzed with overlapping conversations. Someone had set out lemonade and sugar cookies on the long table near the back. The town had thrown weddings in this building, baby showers, Christmas parties, and at least two interventions disguised as potlucks. If there was a reason to gather—and sometimes even when there wasn't—it happened here.

I spotted Ms. Thelma on the stage, perched on her usual stool like she was presiding over the county fair. She was deep in conversation with some of the older residents, people who remembered when the town had only one stop sign and three surnames.

Belle stood beside her, politely nodding. She didn't fit. But somehow she did. Her dress was too crisp, her phone too sleek, her posture too poised. She wore the air of belonging like an old sweater—soft from use, inherited from someone who'd broken it in before her. I couldn't help but think of her mother. Of how natural

Billie would've looked up on that same stage when she came back to town after college. Bo had trailed behind her like a shadow. Like a man content to orbit a sun.

They'd belonged here.

Me? I'd only returned when everything else had run dry.

I stepped farther into the room. The noise folded over me like a quilt. Familiar faces lifted in recognition. Smiles. Nods. Whispers I wouldn't hear until they circled back around to me.

There they were—Tessa, Lana, and Bo—huddled together near the middle of the room. The scene jarred me. It looked to me like they sat at some invisible table I hadn't been invited to, all three of them laughing, grinning, leaning in. The kind of ease that comes from being chosen. Included.

There was no room for me in that little triangle. No extra chair. Not even a sliver of space for my elbows, let alone my heart. I stood at the threshold of it, just far enough away that no one noticed me hovering but close enough to feel the sting.

It was childish, maybe, to feel left out at my age. But I'd spent a lifetime making room for other people. Just once, it would've been nice to have someone save me a seat.

Micah Ellis caught my eye. He gave a wave,

gesturing toward the open chair beside him like it was a front-row ticket to something I hadn't signed up for. I almost went. Almost defaulted to politeness, to whatever version of grace I could muster when I was feeling invisible.

That's when Bo looked up, and everything else dropped away. He smiled like I'd brought sunlight with me. Like I'd walked in and lit the whole damn building. Suddenly it didn't matter if the town didn't have room for me. He did.

Bo stood, still smiling, and lifted a hand in that quiet way of his, calling me over like he knew I was always meant to sit beside him. I went. Like a moth to a warm, steady flame.

He offered me his seat, and when I hesitated— just for a breath, just for the memory of how many times I'd been the one left standing—he bent down and pressed a kiss to my cheek.

Not hurried. Not hidden. A kiss that said, *You belong here. You belong with me.*

I sat in the space he made for me.

"Finally," Tessa said, leaning over and giving me a hug from her seat, grinning at me and then up at Bo. I wasn't sure if the *finally* was about my arrival or my relationship.

"Celia," Lana conceded. She did not offer a hug.

But she had at least acknowledged me without any scorn or sarcasm. So that was a win.

Ms. Thelma called the meeting to order with a gavel that looked like it had been around since the town's founding—and had probably knocked sense into generations of unruly citizens. Or tried to, anyway.

Bo leaned against the wall an arm's length from where I sat, one ankle crossed over the other, arms folded in that easy way of his like he wasn't worried about a damn thing. He looked like sin wrapped in plaid and denim. And oh, the way he kept looking at me—like I was his dessert and he was a man who'd skipped dinner. It didn't do much for my concentration.

Most of the meeting blurred past me in a haze of overly enthusiastic committee members and paper agendas. I clapped politely once or twice along with the crowd during announcements and acknowledgments. But mostly I just let myself sneak glances at Bo.

He caught every single one of them. And didn't look away. His gaze felt like a hand to the small of my back, a whisper against my neck. It was the kind of foreplay you didn't get in a marriage that had long since gone cold. The kind that made you remember you still had a pulse. And hips. And a hell of a lot of unmet needs.

Naturally, that was when Belle said my name. Loudly. Cheerfully. Into a microphone.

"I'm thrilled to announce that we have bestselling author Celia Hart here tonight," Belle said, like she'd just drawn the winning number at a raffle. "Not only will she be signing copies of her books at the Jubilee, she's also agreed to host some writing workshops at Tessa Bloom's yoga studio."

I blinked. Vague memories of being inside Tessa's yoga studio floated back to me. Women wanting to write. Me being volunteered as tribute. That hadn't been finalized. Had it?

There was a beat of silence. Then Darlene Murchison cleared her throat in that pointed, passive-aggressive way she'd perfected on the sidelines at football games. Darlene Murchison had always been the kind of woman who knew how to work a spotlight, even when no one had turned one on.

"Is that really appropriate?" she asked, voice pitched high with sugar and poison. "To showcase books that glorify infidelity and cheating? Is that the kind of message we want to send during a family event?"

Belle looked caught off guard, her mouth opening and closing. She hadn't read any of my books yet. So she didn't know that Darlene was taking the plots way out of context.

Before I could come to my own defense—or pack up and slink out the side door—Lana, of all people, spoke up.

Lana didn't even smooth her skirt or glance at anyone for backup. She just crossed her arms and said, loud enough to carry, "Celia Hart is an award-winning author who's been on bestselling lists Darlene doesn't even know how to pronounce. She's been blurbed by some of the most respected names in publishing and academia. So unless you're suddenly qualified to give a TED Talk on literary merit, I suggest you sit down."

There was a smattering of shocked laughter. Ms. Thelma smacked the gavel again but not very hard this time. Without a squad behind her, Darlene sat. But she continued to mumble under her breath. None of those words reached me since her voice was no longer amplified.

I stared at my former bestie, dumbfounded.

Lana turned toward me then, her expression unreadable. "Only I get to rag on you," she said with a shrug. "It's a seniority thing."

I didn't know what to say. We hadn't been close in a long time. My silence and insecurities had seen to that. Settling into the folding chair with my new boyfriend on my left and my old girlfriends on my right, I realized maybe I wasn't on the outside anymore. Maybe this was the start of my comeback.

CHAPTER TWENTY-THREE

s the meeting wrapped, chairs scraped across the hardwood and people gathered their things in that sluggish way small towns do everything—like maybe if we delayed long enough, someone would announce a nightcap back at their place.

Lana vanished the moment the gavel fell. No goodbye, no sly smile, just gone. But that was fine. She'd done more than enough for me tonight.

Tessa, on the other hand, barreled straight into me with a hug that smelled like lavender lotion and nostalgia. "I'm so proud of you," she whispered into my hair. "And so happy you're finally getting the happily ever after you deserve."

Then she turned to Bo, grinning like a cat who

knew something. "You take care of our girl, Bo Porter."

Bo gave her a mock salute. "Yes, ma'am."

"Details in the morning?"

"Tessa," I laughed. But I was excited about the prospect of sharing bedroom details. Mostly, I was glowing from the *our girl* comment. By the time I'd married Greg, I'd already started losing touch with my girlfriends back home. I hadn't had anyone to share those kinds of details with. Not that Greg did anything worth gossiping over in the bedroom.

The hall didn't empty so much as slowly morph into a receiving line. Neighbors I hadn't spoken to in decades came up like I'd won a trophy and they wanted to touch it. They congratulated me on my books, sure. But they kept glancing at Bo and me, me and Bo. They grinned at us like Bo and I had just announced our engagement or survived a natural disaster. I smiled, nodded, and thanked them for their unsolicited approval.

Bo never left my side. His hand found the small of my back and stayed there. It felt… good. Heavy, in the best way. Like someone was finally holding on to me, not because they needed saving but because they didn't want to let go.

Belle joined us last, her smile wide, her hug quick

but warm. She kissed her father on the cheek, then turned to me.

"I'm heading out with friends," she said. "Dad, take the morning off. Sleep in. Enjoy yourself."

Bo tried to look stern, but it was hard to do with that much fondness in his eyes. "Be safe."

Belle winked at me like we were in on some shared secret and sauntered off in her strappy heels.

And that's when I realized.

They all knew.

Every last one of them. From Thelma to the mayor's cousin to the teenager sweeping up programs. It was in their smirks, their knowing glances, the way no one asked if I'd be coming to Bible study tomorrow. Not that I'd ever gone when I lived here.

They all knew Bo and I were going home together. They all knew exactly what we were going to do. I didn't feel embarrassed. Or exposed. Or like I needed to apologize for being wanted.

I just felt ready.

Outside, the air had cooled just enough to remind me we weren't in high school anymore, even if some part of this night was trying to convince me otherwise. The town hall lights glowed behind us, a soft hum of conversation still floating through the open doors.

Bo slipped his hands into his pockets, looking half-boyish and half-devastating under the lights. "I got a ride here with Belle," he said casually, like it wasn't all part of some elaborate plan to end up exactly where we were now. "Mind giving me a ride home?"

I reached into my purse and fished out my keys. "Sure. Here."

He didn't take them. "I don't mind if you drive."

I curled the keys in my hand, the pointy end digging into my palm. "Greg always had to be the one driving. Even if we were going somewhere I knew better."

Bo's eyes softened. "I'm not Greg. And you're not Billie. We don't have to play by anyone else's rules, Celia. We get to build this our way."

Something warm flickered in my chest. Desire, sure. But it wasn't the heat that gave me pause. It felt like the early glow of something that might one day feel like peace.

The drive was quiet. Not awkward. Comfortable, like slipping into an old robe or drinking a warm cup of tea. When we pulled into Bo's driveway, I

didn't feel nervous. Not like I'd expected. I felt…
present. Whole.

Bo opened the front door of his home and turned to me. "Do you want a glass of wine?"

"No," I said.

"Tea?"

"No."

He smiled like he already knew the answer. "What do you want?"

"You." I wasn't trying to be poetic. I was just tired of asking for less than what I wanted.

Bo crossed the space between us in three easy steps, like he'd been heading my way his whole life. He kissed me like the man he'd grown into—steady, strong, deliberate. There wasn't a single question in it. No hesitation. Just the answer I'd been waiting on.

I kissed him back like someone who was done waiting. Like someone who'd spent a lifetime holding her breath and was finally allowed to exhale. His mouth was warm, familiar in a way that went bone deep, like muscle memory from all of my dreams every night for my whole life.

But then I pulled back, just enough to see his eyes. To make sure this was real. That he was really here. That we both were.

"What are we?" I asked, my breath catching slightly at the edges.

He tilted his head, fingers grazing my cheek. "We are about to make love."

I smiled at the words—*make love*. Not have sex or hook up or blow off steam. There was something old-fashioned in his words, and I loved it. I loved him. But I wasn't ready to tell him that yet.

"I mean, what are we to each other? What is this?"

Bo kissed me again—gentle, then deeper—and when he pulled back, his voice was low and sure. "We're friends. We're about to become lovers. And if I do a good job and get the approval of your girlfriends and half the town for my performance, I'm hoping you'll be mine."

Something in my chest unraveled at those last two words. *Be mine.* As if I were someone worth having.

"Yours?" I asked, already smiling.

"Yeah," he said, like it was the easiest truth in the world. "Mine."

I nodded. "That label works for me."

Bo led me to his bedroom. He didn't rush. He didn't fumble. He didn't act like a man trying to win something. No, he moved like someone who already knew the prize was in the holding.

He undressed me slowly, reverently, as though he understood what this moment cost me to give. As though he knew how long I'd worn this armor and how much trust it took to let it fall away.

He kissed the hollow of my collarbone as he unfastened my shirt, one button at a time. My breath caught when he kissed the soft tip of my breast, gentle as a prayer, before easing my bra from my shoulders. When he dropped to his knees to kiss the stretch of skin just above my navel, I had to close my eyes. Not because I was shy. But because I was afraid I'd cry.

He laid me down gently. He did everything gently with me. For so much of my life, I'd been the strong one. He wasn't handling me like I would break. He was handling me like someone who'd carried too much for too long—and finally deserved to set it all down.

When he started to undress himself, I watched. I wished I were standing. I wanted to kiss every new inch of skin, every quiet history written into his body. But even lying down, my knees were useless things, trembling with anticipation.

We were bare now. Soft in places we used to be

firm. Etched with time. But I'd never seen anything more beautiful in my life than the way he looked and the way he looked at me. Like I was a gift he'd waited decades to unwrap.

I couldn't wait for him to cover me. Touch me. Fill in the lonely places I'd long since learned to ignore.

He pressed against me, his body solid and hot, the blunt weight of him resting low against my belly. There was no mistaking the want between us—his for me, mine for him. We'd already talked about protection and contraception.

His fingers slid between my thighs, testing. I was warm, wanting… but not quite ready. My head and my heart were in the game. My body hadn't gotten the memo that I was eager to let him in. I would've taken the stretch and the sting just to have him sooner. I would've endured the pinch of not being wet enough without complaint, wouldn't have told him to wait.

Bo didn't shove past the part of me that wasn't ready. He stayed right there. With his fingers. Then with his mouth. He worshipped my body like it was holy. Like I was.

By the time he rose over me again, I was no

longer close to ready—I was desperate, writhing, and wet.

My hands were in his hair. His name was a broken plea on my lips. Only then—only when I was open and aching and completely undone—did he enter me.

It didn't feel like being taken. It felt like being returned.

Bo made love to me slowly. He didn't thrust like he was trying to conquer something. He moved with me. Stroke for stroke, breath for breath. It was give and take. Receive and return. A conversation in the language only our bodies remembered, like when we talked out the window or over the fence.

I'd never in my life fought back against a climax. But with him, I didn't want it to end. I wanted to live there, right in the heat of it, in the look in his eyes when he watched me fall apart. But it was a losing battle. Especially when he realized what I was doing.

"Come for me, Cellie."

And I did. I came with a cry, with a sob, with more gratitude than I knew how to speak. He kissed my tears as he followed me over the edge, his body shaking against mine. Then he held me. Tight and close. We caught our breath in the soft silence afterward.

We drifted off tangled together, limbs and breath and warmth. For the first time in my life, I felt… weightless. Like all the years I'd carried, the world had melted off me and pooled in the space between his arms.

There was a sound. A faint buzz. For a second, I thought it was my heart, still fluttering like it had something to say. But it was my phone, somewhere on the nightstand, vibrating against the wood.

I ignored it. Whatever it was could wait. I pressed my face to Bo's chest, let his scent fill my lungs. Heaven, I thought. This is what heaven feels like.

The phone buzzed again.

Then it rang.

I sighed. It was Zach's ringtone. He was probably spiraling over a text that didn't get answered fast enough. Should I let him figure it out on his own? Maybe. Maybe not.

The phone rang again.

I reached for it, peeling myself away from Bo's body with reluctant fingers.

"Mom." His voice was high and tight, stretched like it was holding something back. This was definitely a panic attack. One that I didn't want to deal with right now and—

"Grandpa's not here. I can't find him."

CHAPTER TWENTY-FOUR

I burst through the front door like a woman possessed. My head, which had been in the clouds only moments ago, was thudding. My heart, which had been so calm a doctor might have feared low blood pressure, was pounding in a sharp, panicked rhythm that only family emergencies can summon.

Bo was right behind me. He was calm, but it had no effect on me. Neither did his hand at the small of my back. I barely registered it. The only thing I could hear was the echo of Zach's voice on the phone—"Grandpa's not here. I can't find him."

I took the stairs two at a time, not caring how reckless or undignified it looked. My knees ached in protest, but I didn't stop. Not until I was at the door to my father's room, flinging it open.

The bed was made. Not just made—tucked. Neat hospital corners, like he taught me when I was little. The covers were pulled smooth and tight, his pillow resting precisely in the center. His toothbrush sat in the holder by the sink, damp. Razor put away. Nothing out of place.

I turned and bolted down the stairs again, calling his name though I knew he wouldn't answer. I was still hoping that he was still here. Zach wasn't the best at finding things. My son would say he'd looked for his socks, but I'd ask if he looked with his hands or just his eyes. Then I'd go in and find the socks under some *Magic the Gathering* cards. Please let my dad be hiding underneath a card table.

The backyard was empty. No one was hiding underneath the picnic table. The mint plants swayed in the breeze, the folding chair still facing the sunrise. No coffee cup. No Dad.

I stumbled toward the garage, dread coiling like a snake in my stomach. I didn't want to look. Didn't want to open that door and see—

The car was gone.

I gripped the frame of the doorway, my knuckles gone white. "No," I whispered. "No, no, no."

Bo came up behind me. He'd been in step with me through the entire search.

"He shouldn't be driving. He hasn't even tried in months. The last time he did, he left the car running at the gas station while he walked off to find a Snickers bar."

Bo stepped closer, slow and careful, like I was a spooked animal. "We'll find him."

"They'll take him." My voice cracked. "If we call the police or the hospital or anyone, they'll say I'm unfit. They'll put him in a home and lock the door behind him, and that's it. That's the end."

Bo didn't say anything right away. I finally looked at him, and there it was—the conflict in his eyes. He wanted to argue. He wanted to tell me I was being reckless, or foolish, or irresponsible.

But he didn't. He nodded once, jaw tight. "Then we do it your way."

He turned toward the driveway, already pulling out his phone. "I'll call the girls. Belle, Lana, and Tessa will keep it quiet. Zach and I will split up and check the roads heading west. Maybe he's trying to get to the church, or the store, or—hell, I don't know. Somewhere familiar."

I opened my mouth to say thank you, but my

voice croaked when it came out. "You don't have to do this."

"Of course, I do. You're not alone in this, Celia."

He reached for my hand. I didn't hesitate. I gave it to him. He gave me his strength. His certainty. I felt like I was in one of Zach's video games and the second player just gave me a power up. He held on to me as he made his calls. I soaked in his power as I tried to calm my brain to think. Where would my dad go?

"Belle and Tessa are in. Lana didn't pick up. She's probably in court. I'll fill her in when she calls back."

I nodded, too tight in the chest to speak. Bo pulled Zach into a fast huddle, the three of us standing in a half-circle like we were plotting a heist. We divided up the town—Zach would check the pharmacy, Bo would take the north end where the spring met the creek, and I'd head to the old train station. My father always said that's where he used to wait for my mother before their high school dates. As a kid, I'd imagined it like some kind of black-and-white movie cliché. If his mind had taken him back to then... maybe.

The boys peeled out of the driveway and down the street first. I was halfway to my car, keys clenched in my fist like a weapon, when I heard the unmistakable shuffle of orthopedic soles and the chirp of a voice I did not have the bandwidth for.

"Celia," Ms. Thelma called, tottering toward, clutching a reusable grocery tote. "I was just about to call. I thought I saw a strange man nosing around your garage."

I closed my eyes. I didn't have time for this. We didn't have a neighborhood watch patrol in this town where everybody knew everybody, and crime was limited to petty theft by teens and public drunkenness by coeds.

"He looked like your father, but I didn't think that could be him since we all know he shouldn't be behind the wheel."

A cold, prickling fear crept up my spine. If she knew, then soon the whole town would know in a matter of moments. They'd take my dad. That was if we even found him in time. "Ms. Thelma, maybe mind your own damn business for once."

Her mouth pinched like I'd slapped her. "You watch your tone, young lady. If that was your father, and he was behind the wheel, it is my business. That man's been my neighbor since I was thirteen. I care about him. We all do. We're family here in Stillwater, whether you remember that or not."

I opened my mouth to snap back, but the words

caught on a lump. Tears burned at the backs of my eyes, fast and hot. Before I could stop them, they spilled down my cheeks.

"I'm sorry, Ms. Thelma. Please don't tell. They'll take him away from me, and I'm all he has left."

Ms. Thelma stepped forward and wrapped me up in a hug that smelled like rosewater and decades of tough love. I stood there in her arms, stunned by the warmth of it, and let myself be held.

"You hush that nonsense," she murmured. "You both got a whole town behind you. I'll call my club ladies. We'll find him. We'll bring him home."

I breathed her in, that comforting blend of perfume and porch-swing summers, and for a moment I let the weight of my worries lean into her. I thought of Ms. Thelma and her club ladies, always watching, always knowing, always just a little too involved.

Would that be me and Tessa and Lana one day? In twenty years, sixty-something with matching kaftans and matching opinions, running our mouths and keeping tabs on the whole town?

God help Stillwater if it was. But the thought didn't make me cringe. It made me ache.

I wanted that. I wanted twenty more years of taking care of my father, of sitting on a porch with my friends, of watching these streets and knowing the names of the people who lived on them. I wanted to care, and be cared for, in exactly this way.

My phone buzzed in my hand. I pulled back just enough to check the screen. Then answered on the second ring.

"Lana?"

"Cellie, I have your dad."

My knees buckled with the kind of relief that left bruises. I didn't fall. Ms. Thelma held me up.

CHAPTER TWENTY-FIVE

spotted my father's car the moment I turned onto Main. He'd parked with surgical precision between the yellow lines, as if this cursed disease or old age had never laid a finger on him.

Lana's office was a two-story next to the bakery. Her office was on the second floor, up a narrow staircase that creaked under every step like it had its own opinion. When I stepped inside, I found him seated by the window, sipping from a Styrofoam cup, gaze drifting somewhere beyond the horizon. He looked peaceful. Or vacant. I wasn't sure there was much of a difference anymore.

Lana met me in the hall. She quietly shut her office door behind her, leaving my dad inside. The blinds were open on the glass partition, though, and I could still see him. I could only stare. He looked like my dad, but not quite. Like a house you grew up in that now belonged to someone else.

"He's fine," Lana said. "But you and I need to talk."

I knew that tone. I used to call it her courtroom voice even before she went to law school. The one that made grown men squirm and juries lean in. The one that never let you pretend things were fine when they weren't. I'd first heard it back when we were girls, when Lana stared down a gym teacher twice her size for giving the boys better equipment. I'd heard it when she told her own father to sit down and shut up before he ruined her mother's birthday again. I'd heard it the day she pressed me to go after Bo, argued with me to stop letting Billie steamroll what was between us like I didn't have a say.

That voice didn't rise. It didn't rattle. It cut. Clean and precise, like a scalpel. And if she aimed it at you, it meant she still believed there was something inside worth saving.

"We've always been straight with each other, haven't we?"

I gave a tired nod. "It's why our friendship broke."

Lana didn't take the bait. "I know I'm the friend

people come to when they want the hard truth. And I know you didn't ask me for advice. But the problem showed up at my office door."

"I already know what you're going to say. I don't want to hear it."

"Tough."

I stared past her to my father's profile against the window. The slope of his shoulders. The hollowness of his hands in his lap when he wasn't holding the cup.

"You can't do this, Celia. He needs more care than you can give. You think holding it all together makes you strong. But that's not strength. That's exhaustion wearing a mask."

"You act like you're not the same. Like you're not trying to be Superwoman in heels."

Lana didn't flinch. She nodded. "Yeah. I am Superwoman. And I'm tired, Cellie. I am so goddamn tired because I never get to take off this cape."

Something cracked in me then. A split so quiet it didn't make a sound, but I felt it—like a hairline fracture running through my ribs. Not pain. Just... release.

I saw her then. Not the grown woman in the designer suit and expensive heels. I saw the girl she used to be behind her makeup.

When had we stopped being girls? Had we ever really been carefree children? I tried to picture us without the weight. No expectations, no responsibilities. Just sunburnt shoulders and too-loud laughter. But I couldn't summon it. It felt like we'd come out of the womb with our spines already braced, already carrying things too heavy for us. Probably a genetic trait—passed in utero from our mothers, who never got to be girls either.

I couldn't remember the last time I felt weightless. No, that's not true. It was last night in Bo's arms. When the world went quiet and I didn't have to hold anything but him.

Before that, it was with Tessa. When she'd wrapped me up in that hug back at Spice & Sundries. That one caught me off guard. I hadn't expected it to land so deep.

But that was the thing about being seen, truly seen. It peeled the years right off you. For a breath, for a heartbeat, I'd been just a girl again. A girl who didn't have to be strong. A girl who got to be held.

I opened my arms.

For a second, Lana just looked at me. Like she didn't trust the invitation. Or maybe didn't remember how to accept one. Like the idea of being held felt foreign.

Then she stepped forward and let me pull her in. Her body was stiff at first, like she didn't know what to do with softness. But she sank into it, slow and heavy, like someone who hadn't rested in years.

I held her. Not because I had the answers. Not because I was strong enough to carry her weight. I held her because she'd carried mine more times than I could count. Because she needed it right now. Because I did too.

We held each other like women who'd both come too close to the edge. Like we could brace each other just long enough to step back. We didn't cry. The silence was full enough. This was what forgiveness looked like between two tired women—bone-weary and bruised by the lives we'd held up too long.

Moments later, I stepped into the office, the door clicking shut behind me like the punctuation mark on the conversation I didn't want to have.

My dad didn't look up. He just sat there, hands wrapped around the cup of coffee like it was the last thing tethering him to the moment. But I knew he was in there. I knew that version of him still lived somewhere beneath the haze.

"Dad…" I started.

He raised a hand. Steady. Clear-eyed. And for a second, I was sixteen again, caught sneaking back in after curfew. That hand could still stop me in my tracks.

"Don't," he said. His voice was rough, but not confused. Not today. "I need to say something before you go turning yourself inside out to save me."

I opened my mouth, but the words got stuck somewhere behind my ribs. So I just nodded.

"I'm not myself, Celia. I know what's happening. I forget names. Places. The other day I looked in the mirror and didn't recognize my own damn face. Thought someone broke in to shave and steal my toothbrush."

I swallowed hard.

"And this morning, I drove here... but I don't remember leaving the house. I only knew I was going somewhere. When I came back to myself, that scared the hell out of me."

He looked up then. Right at me. No fog. Just the man who raised me, steady and sharp and trying not to tremble.

"I could've hurt someone. I could've hurt you." His voice cracked. "And that... that's not how I want this to go. That's not who I want to be."

"Dad," I whispered, but it wasn't enough.

"I've been thinking about it for a while. I didn't want to say it because I know how much you've already given up. I'm going back into the care facility."

"Daddy—" It was all I could say.

"Baby girl, this"—he gestured at the Styrofoam cup, at himself, at everything unraveling in quiet, invisible ways—"this is the best way I can take care of you."

My knees buckled before my pride could stop them. I dropped into the chair beside him and buried my face in his shoulder like I hadn't done since Mom died.

My father held me. Stronger than I expected. Still my dad, even as the pieces fell apart.

We didn't say much after that. Just let the silence stretch around us. Heavy. Healing. Whole in all the places we'd been breaking.

I didn't know how long I cried. But when it was done, I wasn't holding on to grief anymore. I was holding on to him.

CHAPTER TWENTY-SIX

Tessa leaned up into the front seat like she used to when we were teenagers. Chin propped on the back of her hand, elbow on the console. Eyes crinkled with mischief reflected back at her in the rearview mirror. "Remember when you drove us to the mall that summer and we made you park two rows over so no boys would know we came with a parent, Mr. H?"

Dad chuckled from the passenger seat. "I got sunstroke waiting in that car. I should've let you find out the hard way what it's like to walk home in July with blistered feet and no sense of direction."

"Oh, we knew where we were going," Tessa said. "Right to the food court to flirt with the guy at Orange Julius."

"Tony Petito," Lana and I said in unison.

We all laughed. It was a good day. A good memory day all around. Memories of the past. Memories still held in the present. It wasn't about memory loss or care homes or what came next. We were all back living in the late '80s. I was still someone's daughter, someone's best friend, still full of possibility.

Dad had spent the night at home, awash in memories. In the morning, he was still himself. But we knew better than to rely on that. We packed up and headed to the care facility. This time was different.

The first time he went to the care home, he'd only taken a shaving kit, a few changes of clothes, and a few pictures of me and Mom. He hadn't planned to stay. Hadn't packed like someone settling in. More like someone riding out a storm. Temporary shelter, not surrender.

But now…

Now he packed like a man moving house. Not a suitcase but boxes. Sturdy ones, the kind you save from appliance deliveries and tuck in the garage just in case. I found him in the den wrapping framed photos in dish towels, stacking them next to his slippers and the quilt Mom had stitched back before her hands gave out. He even labeled them. Closet things. Books. Desk drawer—keep.

I stood there in the doorway, watching him fold his sweaters with the same precision he once used to fold my school permission slips. And I realized this wasn't a trip. Not a weekend visit or a summer stay. This was the long haul.

My girlfriends had shown up and piled into the backseat like the old days. Lana brought coffee and that no-nonsense energy that had once gotten us into trouble and now got us out of it. Tessa had snacks and sage to ward off lingering spirits in my dad's new room. They hadn't asked if I wanted company. They just showed up, like they used to do for me. Like we used to do for each other. With them in the backseat—my girls, my people—it didn't feel like a loss. It felt like a send-off. Like family.

The building that housed the care facility loomed up in front of us. Polished. Respectable. It had that sanitized calm meant to soothe visiting family more than the residents themselves. I pulled into the loading zone, shifted the car into park, and exhaled.

"I guess this is it," Dad muttered, but he didn't make a move to unbuckle. "Kind of like when I dropped you off at college."

"Except I'm going to visit every day."

"Don't cramp my style, baby girl."

"Ohhhh, Mr. H! Are you planning to start dating?" asked Tessa.

"You never know. I read some articles about what goes on in senior homes."

"Well, just make sure to strap up," said Lana.

"Lana!" I covered my face.

My father just chuckled and unbuckled his seatbelt. We all climbed out of the car. My friends came around and gave my dad hugs in turn.

"We'll be here," Tessa said, reaching forward to squeeze his shoulder. "You're not getting rid of us. We'll be loitering around here like bored teenagers by next week."

Dad laughed. Then he turned to me, eyes full of something I couldn't name—maybe gratitude, maybe grief, maybe both—and kissed my temple like he used to every morning before school.

I nodded, not trusting my voice, and walked with him to the front where Dr. Ellis waited. My father offered his hand like a gentleman. I handed him over like a mother sending her child off to his first day of school. Maybe that's what this was—full circle in the cruelest, most loving way.

As they turned down the hall, Dr. Ellis looked back at me.

"You know, Celia," he said, "I'd still like to take you out sometime."

"I don't think my boyfriend would appreciate that."

His brow lifted. "You and Bo Porter, huh?"

"Yeah. Me and Bo Porter."

"Took you two long enough."

Outside, the air felt lighter. Or maybe I did. I slid back into the driver's seat and pulled out of the lot. Tessa reached over to turn on the radio. Lana put down the window and rolled her hand like a wave into the wind. For one blessed stretch of road, it felt like we could outrun the years.

"So," Lana said, her voice sharp with glee, "you and Bo Porter?"

Tessa gasped, clutching invisible pearls. "Tell us everything."

"How big is it?"

"More importantly, does he know what to do with it?"

I sucked my teeth as I came to a stop sign on Main. "In the words of Meg Ryan, *Yes, Yes, Yes!*"

"All right, Bo!" cheered Tessa.

"I want some of what she's having," sighed Lana.

I gripped the wheel, preparing to press on the gas when I heard the whoop of a siren. Seriously?

The blue and red lights flashed in my rearview. I sighed as I pulled over to the curb. A moment later, the same officer from before—the one who'd pulled me over on my first day back, I still didn't remember his name—stepped out of his cruiser like he had something to prove.

"Ma'am," he said, peering into the car, "you came to a full stop, but you remained there longer than is necessary. That's considered—"

"Officer Vincent," Lana cut in, leaning forward from the passenger seat, her voice cool as glass and just as sharp. "Are you really about to write a ticket for obeying the law a little too well?"

Vincent? No. It couldn't be Mark Vincent, the guy I'd kinda dated back in high school?

He blinked. Yup, that was the same dumbfounded look he'd given me when I didn't let him get to second base. "Well, I—"

"Because I'm fairly certain that would not hold up in court. Or in front of a reporter. Or in front of your supervisor, who I happen to know personally."

Officer Vincent looked at her. Then at me. Then back to Lana. His gaze lingered on Lana as though recognizing her trumped picking on me. "Just a warning."

"Smart choice," Lana said, settling back in her seat like a queen who'd just spared a subject.

The squad car pulled off. I stared after it, then shook my head and laughed.

Tessa let out a whoop and smacked my shoulder. "Look at us, getting warnings and getting laid."

I pulled back onto the road, the sun spilling gold across the dash, and I couldn't stop smiling. It felt like the band was back together. Me and my two best friends, exactly as it was supposed to be.

CHAPTER TWENTY-SEVEN

When I walked into the house, I braced for the usual: shoes where they didn't belong, dishes breeding in the sink, and that subtle smell of boy funk that lingered in the air like an uninvited guest. Instead, the place was… neat. Tidy. Respectable, even.

Zach stood near the kitchen, his posture a little too casual, like he was trying not to seem proud of himself. But I could see it. The way his chest lifted just a bit. How he was waiting for me to notice.

And I did. Not just the gleaming counters or the absence of dishes in the sink, but him. It jarred me. He didn't look like his father. There was something in the line of his jaw, the set of his shoulders, that pulled me back. Not to my ex. To my dad.

Zach had my father's quiet dignity. That same deep stillness that made people lean in to listen. I respected my dad more than any man in this world. Zach had his flaws, but standing there, looking more like his grandfather than I'd ever noticed before, I saw the man he might still grow into.

"I cleaned up," he said, shrugging one shoulder. "Figured you had enough on your plate."

There was a time I might've cried over that small kindness. A time I might've snarked. But today, I just nodded and said, "Thank you." Because it mattered. And I didn't want to ruin it by reaching for too much.

"Oh, and I got a job," he added. "Part-time. Stocking at the hardware store for now, but I'm applying to other places. Stuff that fits more with my skills."

My eyes landed on the sketchbook open on the table. A half-finished piece stretched across the page in bold, aching lines. Zach always drew emotion better than he spoke it. I used to think he'd be a famous illustrator or animator. I didn't push for that career path now. I smiled, nodded, and didn't try and pave or plow anything out his way.

There was a knock at the door. Bo and Belle stood on the porch like a Hallmark postcard. Belle had takeout bags in both hands and a grin that could crack stone.

"Dinner delivery," she said. "Dad said this is your favorite. I remain unconvinced that it is edible."

Belle held out the bag from Spice & Sundries like it was radioactive. "I brought curried tofu for me, curried chicken for Zach. You and Dad can fight over the rest."

Zach stepped in, visibly lighting up. Until she added, "We've got to look out for each other now that our parents are dating. You know, since we're practically siblings."

I watched my son's face fall, that brief spark flicker out behind his eyes. He recovered quickly, but I caught it. I always caught it. Just like my dad used to catch it in me.

Belle breezed past, setting the food on the table. Her gaze landed on the sketchbook.

"Is this yours?" she asked.

Zach nodded, suddenly looking like he'd been caught naked in public. He moved to shut the sketchbook.

"No—wait," Belle said. "It's good. Like, really good. Have you ever done any graphic design? I could use someone for the Jubilee materials. Flyers. Social stuff. Maybe the website?"

Zach stammered something unintelligible. Belle kept talking. They leaned in toward each other, two young people caught in the spark of new possibility, even if only one of them knew it.

Bo slid closer to me, brushing his hand against mine. His thumb stroked the back of my hand like he was memorizing me.

"I missed you today," he said.

I looked up at him. The tenderness in his face nearly undid me.

"How'd things go with your dad?"

I let out a slow breath. "Better than I thought they would. Worse than I wanted them to."

He nodded, like he understood every unspoken word in between. "You want to spend the night at my place?"

"Yeah. I'd like that."

Because for once, there was nothing to fix. Just someone to hold me when the day was done.

I finally had someone to hold me, many someones. My girlfriends had my back. My son was pulling his weight. My dad was getting help so that we could be there for each other at this stage in our lives. And then there was Bo. All he wanted to do was hold me —preferably horizontally.

And he did. We lay in a bed wide enough for two

and the time to tangle our limbs until we forgot where one ended and the other began. His hand was warm against my hip, his breath steady at my neck. I'd spent a lifetime bracing, anticipating, holding it all together. Now I was letting go, inch by inch, under the weight of a man who only ever wanted to hold me.

Bo's chest rose and fell beneath my cheek, the rhythm steady, grounding. I traced a slow circle over the bare skin just above his heart, listening to the faint echo of us still in the room—our breaths, the soft creak of the old bed frame, the silence that came after all that wonderful exertion.

"I'm so damn happy we're here," he said, voice low and warm, roughened at the edges. "You were worth the wait."

I swallowed. The words landed somewhere deep, where I didn't have defenses built. "I'm still working on myself."

"That's fine. I'll just do what I always did when we were young: sit quietly beside you while you work."

He had done that. He'd sat in the backyard beside me as I read. Sat in the library beside me as I wrote. He'd always been beside me ...until I ran. I would never make that mistake again.

"I'll be your silent cheerleader, Cellie. Your unpaid intern. Your emotional support lumberjack."

I laughed, letting my forehead rest against his shoulder.

"And I'll always save my pickle for you." He rubbed his semi-hard cock against my thigh.

That made me snort. "God, Bo."

He grinned, shameless. I shook my head, smiling into his skin. Then he grew serious.

"I'll hold your hand when you visit your dad," he said, quieter now. "I'll hang with your son, even though he's grown. And at night…" His lips brushed my temple. "At night, I'll fuck you into oblivion."

I closed my eyes. Let myself lean into it, into him.

"That sounds like the perfect life."

Bo kissed the crown of my head like a promise. "It's the happily ever after we both deserve."

Want to read Lana's story?
Check out *Still Got It*
at JemJohnsonBooks.com

ABOUT THE AUTHOR

Jem Johnson writes small-town, big-heart romances about women over forty rediscovering desire, purpose, and the power of second chances. A firm believer that it's never too late to fall in love—or finally choose yourself—Jem crafts emotionally rich stories filled with family ties, lifelong friendships, and slow-burn chemistry that simmers through every season of life. When she's not writing, you'll find her people-watching in a coffee shop, filling her planner with too many stickers, or plotting her next fictional Jubilee. *Stillwater Springs* is her love letter to women who've done the work… and are ready to feel alive again.

Visit my web store for steals, deals, and access to my books before they're on retailers! https://jemjohnsonbooks.com/

ALSO BY JEM JOHNSON

STILLWATER SPRINGS

Still the One

Still Got It

Still Healing

Still Mine

Still Yours

Still Home

* 9 7 8 1 9 5 4 1 8 1 8 2 3 *